The Writer

Kate Sparrows

Kate Sparrows; kate.sparrows@gmail.com
https://www.facebook.com/kjsparrows

Publisher's Note: This is a work of fiction. Names, characters, places, and incidents are a product of the author's imagination. Locales and public names are sometimes used for atmospheric purposes. Any resemblance to actual people, living or dead, or to businesses, companies, events, institutions, or locales is completely coincidental.

Cover Design: Kassi Jean Formatting & Design
Printed by CreateSpace, An Amazon.com Company

The Writer/ Kate Sparrows. -- 1st ed.
ISBN 978-1-943797-09-7

"Most people have to get to a point where they don't have a choice before they'll change something."

— Alex Marwood

Chapter One

Adam sat on the bed beside me, leaning against the headboard, while I was sprawled upside down on my stomach. I knew what he was thinking. It was finally Friday night, but this week was hell. It was always hell for me, but Adam got sucked into my brimstone a little more this time. He was the guy dating the freak.

"Hailstorm," he sighed, using my pet name. "It would be so much easier if I was like you. We could get out of this backwards town and just make it, ya know. Just you and me out on our own"

It wasn't anything I hadn't heard before. Adam thought having this... ability, was great. It sucked most of the time. I actually had to do hours of research on the simplest homework assignments. I actually had to know shit. Sure, I'd never get a history question wrong on a test... but that's how Genghis Khan accidently had a sex change to be Genny Han: Ruler of the Silken Trail and Murdering Provocateur. That was one mistake that got creative to fix. Who knew blood splatter could make such elegant upholstery for the British Queen? Yes, the royal family had an already bloody history but I accidentally added to the horror of that. There are some fashion choices a girl can just not forget.

With what I could do, there were rules and guidelines. Sure, Adam had seen enough of the reasons why over the five years we've been together. But there were still things I didn't know if he could handle. He'd never be normal again. Trust me, I've tried. Somehow those words meant nothing.

"Haley... Haley... Haley... Haley... Haley..."

Okay, so there was no ignoring him this time. Maybe it was because graduation was coming up and he was worried college would split us if he didn't get into UConn with me. Adam was lucky to get into Northeastern, and it was only a few hours' drive to my second choice school.

"Haley. Haley. Haley. Haley. Haley."

I rolled over onto my back and stared up at his stupid smirking face. I had to give him credit – he knew how to get to me. Adam already had the puppy-dog face ready and it sure made it hard to say no to his baby blues. But that didn't mean I wouldn't give in so easily. It might actually be nice having someone else like me around, which always was a thought I had every other time things sucked.

"What?" I laughed.

He just shook his head and sat up to lean over me, his face inches from mine. "Make me like you."

"Okay."

"Please... wait, what?" Those baby blues blinked fast behind the dark hair that fell across his face. He was asking me if I was serious, if I was joking. All I was thinking about was that he needed to cut that mop of hair if he wanted any shot at a summer job this year. Then again I could just make that happen anyways, even though he's said he never wanted me to write about him. He said he was happy earning less as a lifeguard because it let him work on his tan and play hero. I was going to intern at the bank and make a real living this summer.

"Are you serious?" Was I?

I nodded and rolled onto my side when he got off the bed to dig around my backpack for a notebook or some kind of scrap paper. It was like he knew that if something wasn't put into my hands soon that I'd back out. But there wasn't much in there anymore with school ending. Just my track uniform and sneakers.

"Adam, there's something you should know." I knew I could have gotten away with going through the motions of writing things out. He would have seen the words on the paper and knew I did my best. He knew that was how it worked and, yet, he would be powerless. "It's going to hurt... a lot." But there was a chance it would work.

He paused in his fruitless search, standing upright. "What ya mean, Hailstorm?"

A superhero name for someone who was not a superhero. It wasn't like I had a great backstory or some sweet way I got this way. What I wouldn't give to have just been bitten by a bug or to have been born like this! The thing was that I really didn't know exactly why this happened to me. I just remembered waking up and being alone. I was the only one able to see my parents after that and they always looked a bit different. Guess that's one of the side effects of being in a fatal car crash – the whole being dead thing. But it was probably just a seven-year-old's mind coping with tragedy to imagine up ghosts existing. I didn't want to make Adam one too.

"I'm this way because of what happened to my parents." Drunk driver. Broad daylight. Three dead, and me in a coma. I was the "oops" baby but I was sure glad to have an older sister, even if she was old enough to be my mom if she had gotten knocked up by her high school boyfriend. Then again, he was a douche and I'm so glad Jen didn't put out for that weasel.

The bed dipped and it knocked me out of my thoughts. I shouldn't be stuck on the past. It happened and it was over with. It wasn't like I could rewrite it without making things a hundred times worse. And I doubt it was my worried and depressed feelings I was seeing mirrored in Adam's eyes. There was something else on his mind and it seemed like whatever it was had made him, maybe, reconsider.

"Do my parents have to die too?" His voice got quiet at the end and he looked away. It was like he hated himself for wanting this, or maybe he hated me a little for what I paid for it. Not that I had a choice.

It was the first time I heard such regret and pain in his voice. Adam was insanely close to his parents. Even his crazy little kid brother, Ian, who drove him crazy and always seemed to walk in on Adam – naked – in the bathroom. The thought of losing his parents was something Adam wouldn't be able to handle. It was something no one our age should have to even think about. I also wasn't asking him to give up his family. Not if I could write it so he'd never hurt or lose them. I didn't want him to lose his parents either. They kind of because my adoptive parents when Adam and I started dating. Even though I had Jen, there were times when she just wanted to do her own thing and have a life. April and Ken Montgomery were the nicest folks in this town.

Sitting up, I turned his face back towards me. "Hey." His eyes still lingered off to the side. "Buttface, look at me." Okay, there was half of a chuckle. "It's a legit question, but no. I don't think this has anything to do with them." No, what it did have to do with just sucked.

"I don't think they have to be there. I mean, mine were only there because what seven-year-old is allowed to joy ride a Studebaker around Applegate?" Although I probably could have gotten pretty far before my stubby little legs would have needed to hit the brakes. I've gotten lucky before on the drive to school and missed all by one red light through town.

"Then what, Hailstorm? How could this hurt me?"

How could it hurt him when I could write away his pain? The worst part was that I couldn't. That might be part of this whole thing and this wasn't going to happen twice even if Adam wanted it to. How do you explain to the cops that it's just a coincidence to be innocent in two car crashes that happen the exact same way? You can't. Then dating me made it worse if they connected the dots to my parents. Some poor schmuck helping Adam would take the fall over nothing he'd ever done. No, one try was all he was getting, like ever.

"You'd be in a car crash..." Wow, it was hard to face someone and say horrible things. I found my bottom lip between my teeth as I fought how I wanted to break the news. I mean, I didn't really have to tell him everything.

Shit, if I didn't love him so much I wouldn't be trying to talk him out of this or even caring if he ended up dead or maimed or a vegetable. Then again, we probably wouldn't be having this talk and I wouldn't be thinking of his battered and bloody body in a hospital bed – cuts all over his face and blood matting his hair; his mother crying at his bedside; his father wanting to kill me for letting this happen.

"Oh." *Yea.* "How bad?"

Shit.

He hadn't given this up. I didn't want to relive all I went through just to tell him exactly how bad it was. I only knew what the pain was like a week later when I woke up. By then I had been in and out of surgery, doped up on pain killers, and healing. But it was still hell.

"Very bad. Remember that time we went skiing and you broke your arm?" Adam nodded. That was a painful experience he'd remember. "It's like that but with every bone in your body broken all at once and then set on fire. Your brain gets bounced around and scrambled so much that just thinking hurts. Nobody tells you that, but they're all begging for you to say something so they know you're alright."

Okay, so there were still bitter memories there. I'd have to tone it down a little and not let it build on my emotions from this week. Adam needed facts. "You'll want to die when you wake up from the coma." Yea, totally leaving out the emotions...

When I finally risked looking at him, his gaze drifted off a little towards my bookcase in the corner. It was hard to read his face to know where his mind was right now. The only worse than a coma was death. Shit was serious.

"Adam, I'll forget this ever came up. Let's go down to Del's and get lemonade."

It was strange that he didn't move. Del's frozen lemonade was the bomb. It was the only thing that made New England tolerable in the summer if you were miles from the beach. Adam was more addicted to the stuff than I was. Yet there was no reaction when I nudged him.

"I want to do this."

There went the last of the air from my "It's All Ok" balloon. Maybe I didn't see how serious he was before or maybe I just failed to talk him out of it. It was like going to Del's and then being told you couldn't have any. Doing this was letting Adam down. He just couldn't see that.

"Haley, I don't think I could live with myself if something happened to my parents though," he said quietly. "You got to promise me that they'd be alright." His eyes even refused to look at me. I don't know if it was because his mind already put the blame on me or if Adam was feeling guilty about the slightly callous remark and *my* parents. I survived... somehow.

But with all our grandiose plans, Adam was forgetting the part of that plan that would really devastate his parents. I knew I could just pretend it hadn't crossed my mind. I mean, Adam was almost eighteen and an adult. It wasn't like he needed his parents or anyone to tell him what to do. And I should *finally* be able to have something I wanted for a change; I gave up enough. I wanted us just to go to college together. I wanted it just to be the two of us and, with him being normal, it wasn't

12

like it was something we wouldn't be able to work through. It wasn't really permanent if we didn't get into the same college either. Sure it might feel permanent, but there were cell phones and email and stuff. It wasn't like it would be goodbye forever. But I was stalling and rambling instead of just coming out with it.

"You know, if we leave and get out of here, that you gotta say goodbye to them... right?" I doubted that he even thought about that. He didn't flinch or react at all. Maybe he definitely didn't think it out. I hated that I had because I always had to think things through. "They're not going to understand why we want to leave. They won't know you're different and maybe they won't be able to understand you or let you around Ian."

Okay, maybe I was less pointing out the obvious thorn in his plan and more trying to stop him from going down this road, my road. But maybe I was the problem in all this. Maybe Adam thought he needed to completely change.

I reached over and took his hand. I still couldn't believe he was zoned off and refusing to look at me. "Adam, I love you the way you are. We're going to be together forever. What you'd be giving up for me isn't worth it. We'll just wait until we graduate and then leave together." I ran my thumb softly back and forth over the top of his hand. "You don't have –"

"I won't be able to have your back," he cut me off. It was such a weird thing to say. Why'd he need to have my back? He already had my back. Adam was there at school and helped me get through everything. I wanted to ask what in the world he meant, but he continued. "If something uncontrollable happens, I want to be able to stop it and save you. And it's not going to be fair if you write out everything we ever need and give me some messed up backwards fairytale; or worse, you play normal and we both struggle together. I want to be able to give you the world. You deserve that much and more, Haley. I just want to be man enough for you."

Oh, Adam...

"But you are." Only he wasn't having it.

Adam got up and walked to the other side of the room, his hand running through his hair as he looked around my desk. He wasn't taking my words and letting me smooth things over. He wasn't just going along and seeing that I could handle it. Somehow Adam knew I was worried. Somehow he knew I desperately wanted someone else like me to be around and to understand the messed up life fate threw in my face. It isn't fair of me to want that from Adam, no matter how much I love him. It wasn't fair that he wasn't thinking about himself during the hugest decision of his life that he'd ever make. It sucked that I couldn't reason with him. I failed in not fighting harder to protect who he was... and guilty because I wanted this, even if I didn't want to be the reason he went through all the pain.

I forced myself off the bed and walked up behind him. I knew I had already just agreed to doing this, even though I was the only one trying to continually back out. I loved Adam with everything I had. If he dropped to one knee to propose, I wouldn't spare a second in telling him that I'd spend the rest of my life as his. This really was no different when you really – really – thought about it.

Wrapping my arms around his waist, I let my face be buried in his back before resting my cheek against his shoulder. "It's going to take me some time to think it all out and get the words right. I don't think your mom would be happy if you missed spaghetti night while I sat around thinking how to write."

I felt his body sag. It was probably out of relief that he knew without a doubt I was writing him. Maybe it was just getting late and the talk of dinner reminded him of that. I knew I'd be sighing and collapsing on the bed after all this emotional stuff.

"Haley, it's going to be okay." I hadn't expected him to say that. In fact, Adam said it so quietly that I thought I imagined it at first. "You're doing the right thing... *We're* doing the right thing."

Adam made me believe him. Even if it was just for a moment... I still felt horrible over what was going to come. I had lived through it and there were some things that you just didn't wish upon another human being. Not even the bitchy ones that made your life a living hell.

He turned in my arms and tipped my head up to look at his. How could there not be any worry or conflict or anything in those baby blues? Adam seemed so sure and set. I really needed that strength he had. Maybe he knew it. Maybe that was even more reason to have him at my side forever.

"I'll try to make it hurt as little as possible, Adam. I promise." Crap, my voice was trembling so much that I might as well have been crying too.

His lips gently pressed against mine for a moment that was way too short. "I know, Hailstorm." He kissed me again, letting it linger just a little bit longer.

I didn't want to let him go. It seemed so irrational when I knew I'd see him again tomorrow. And afterwards, I'd be able to see him every day that he was in the hospital, even if he may never know I was there because of the coma. But I would know and knowing I never left him was all that mattered. I could still touch him and hold his hand and kiss him. I'd just have to wait to hear his voice and see those baby blues is all.

"Call me before you go to bed," I begged. I knew it was silly but I just needed to talk to him again. I needed to know I could make it through what I was about to do. I needed to reassure him that he'd make it through this okay and I needed him to reassure me that he would. I needed to be able to tell him and force him to know how much I love him and that I'd be waiting.

He kissed me one last time before heading towards my bedroom door. "Promise."

Adam smiled as he picked up his backpack off the floor. He dug out his keys and shoved them in his pant pocket before coming back to steal one more kiss.

"Don't look so sad, Hailstorm. You're going to be stuck with me for the rest of your life." He chuckled. Yea, maybe it would be funny one day but it was just too soon. Too much had to be gotten through before I could really laugh at that notion. Too much I had to sit down and do. And too much pressure on my shoulders at the moment.

I watched him leave, giving him a small wave as he headed down the stairs by my room and walked out the front door. My mind kept drifting to bad things and it was freaking annoying right now. I just wanted to think the best and have a clear head going into this. It wouldn't be hard to slip in the idea that after he woke up and was healed that he'd take me to Costa Rica on a whim and elope in some grand wedding on the beach. Adam might even think he dreamt it up in his coma. Yea, a beach wedding would be fun.

It barely kept a smile on my face as I dug out my beaten up journal. I knew it was something I should be taking better care of, given what I could do. But it was probably because of what I could do that it was that way. I had to take my anger – initially – out on something. I flipped to the back and found a spot where there were a couple empty pages. Hopefully that would be enough.

What wasn't enough were the waves of inspiration smacking my brain as I lightly tapped the side of my head with the purple polka dotted pencil. I was drawing a blank. I knew that I needed to get him into a car and that there needed to be a car crash that landed him in a coma. I think Jen had said I had a concussion and bleeding on the brain. That or she used it only as a backhanded nice comment to call me stupid and dumb and retarded. Normal sibling crap.

Adam gets into his car and puts on his seat belt. He puts his favorite music on and starts driving out of town. He's calm and relaxed as he drives. There's no one on the road as he heads towards the county line.

I knew that would be the best place for this "accident" to occur. The crossroads where the main road from Applegate met the main road from Hillsborough. Both towns would get the call seeing as it was on county land. Both towns would send their ambulances down these highway roads and there was no way Adam would accidentally be missed. The response time would be pretty quick. He'd get the bump on his head and be recovering at the hospital in no time. Making sure he put on his seat belt would protect him from any major injuries. Hopefully he wouldn't get too cut up from any broken glass...

His car goes off the road and he crashes. The windshield of his car is shattered, but none of the glass cut his face or leaves large cuts on his body.

Well, that was one way to ensure he didn't get too banged up, but now for the hard part. How was I going to make sure what needed to happen to him happened?

It was tempting to write that I suddenly received an email with the details of my crash and the medical reports from the hospital. That would definitely raise up some unwanted red flags. No one could know that he was different and no one could link it back to me and know my secret. Besides, that would take too much time to happen. Guess it was going to take the old fashion way to survive.

I got up and headed over to my desk to boot up the ancient monster on my desk. The dial-up tones of the internet were enough to make me cringe. I swear this computer was older than me, but it was my parents' and held a special place in my heart. Yea... but it really was just what we had and it was free. Like Jen liked to remind me: beggars can't be choosers. I was stuck with this until I figured out a way to get something better, minus writing for one on a whim. Jen would lecture me about abusing my power and then take the computer away in the end. Too much hassle.

I double-clicked the E-looking logo and waited for the homepage to come up. I don't know how anyone had been able to stand these slow speeds. Everyone that waited around for this dinosaur must have turned grey and died off... or walked away and got on with their life until technology finally caught up.

It loaded at last and let me bring up my favorite search engine. It was sickening that it took my computer a minute and a half to load the screen but the internet was dissected and picked about for my search query and was sitting waiting for me after only 0.94 seconds. There were only four articles. Two were of the crash. One was my parents' obituary. The last was one about me being in the hospital, so it sounded from the headline. I clicked the last one first.

The story wasn't nothing more than three lines. I had woken up from my coma as an orphan from a crash that still was under investigation. Jen was to be granted fully custody over me. Although, it that wasn't true in the real world. There was my grandma for a little while before she passed on and then one uncle that popped up in my memories every once in a while. Lots of babysitters though. I definitely remember them more than my own family.

Chapter Two

"At eight fifty-three on the morning of February 25th, Adam Russel Montgomery was involved in a fatal vehicle crash. He was the sole occupant when he lost control of the vehicle on County Line Road. The vehicle swerved, striking a utility pole. There were no witnesses.

"County forensics explains the horrific accident. High voltage transmission wires fell on the vehicle after it struck and splintered the utility pole. Impact caused a leak of oil and/or brake fluid that caused a fire to originate under the engine compartment with a spark from the downed electrical line. Fire was found to have engulfed the entire vehicle when maintenance crews arrived to fix the reported electrical outage. Montgomery was trapped within the blaze and pronounced dead on the scene when emergency personal arrived.

"Adam Montgomery was a senior at Applegate High School and participated on the track team, helping bring AHS to State Finals last year. A bright student, loved by all, Montgomery was accepted to Northeastern University's Mechanical Engineering Program.

"A memorial service will be held at the Montgomery home on Friday from 3pm – 6pm. Counselors will be on site at AHS this week to help with this tragic loss."

I couldn't read anymore of Adam's obituary. I just kept the news article mostly for his photograph.

The accident had happened just a few months before our graduation. Ha! Accident... like it could really be called that. It was my fault. Might as well just say he was murdered by his "loving girlfriend, Haley Brown", as the local newspaper obituary had put it. I was the one that didn't think of the chances that his seat belt would malfunction and trap him in the car. I was the one that didn't think of the chances that he'd hit the utility pole and snap a wire that would set his car on fire. I was the one that didn't think of the chances that no one would have come around for hours if it wasn't for the big high school football game was on TV and the power outage happening in the middle of it to have enough Applegate residents complain. I was the one that didn't see it wasn't foolproof.

I let him down. I murdered Adam.

Jen had forced me to finish the year and walk across the graduation stage. She kept pointing out that I was already considered graduated with my grades and how far into the year it was – all I had to do was show up. But everyone at school suddenly seemed so caring, too caring. I couldn't even use the restroom without being consoled about my loss, and reminded that I killed him. Every person that ever bullied me even turned nice and wanted to be there for me. The teachers just wrote me passes for everything and basically removed the promised distraction of homework and exams. Not that I could have focused on any schoolwork at that point.

It was the actual ceremony that I feared the most. I would be walking alone and moving on with my life, getting out of that small town, but Adam would not. I'd be leaving him behind. At first, Jen understood. Then she started pushing me when graduation got closer. She said I would regret not going and I would put the blame and hate on Adam. If only she knew what I had done. I had burned those pages right after I found out he was gone for good.

I was supposed to walk across that graduation stage and make new memories. I was in tears before I even made it up the three small steps. I turned and ran out of the auditorium's side door while Jen made plans to pick up my graduation certificate and decided what kind of lecture she was going to give me for bolting mid-ceremony. I knew I couldn't go to Northeastern and try to live for Adam, and I didn't want to go to UConn without him. But I knew I just couldn't stay here either.

I had ran out to the playground near our house after graduation. Climbing up into the little hut at the top of the slide, I felt safe just like I had all those nights spent talking to Adam. It was the place he first kissed me. If any place had enough magic to bring Adam back to life, it was this place.

Adam Montgomery is alive.

Adam Montgomery survived the crash.

Adam Montgomery never was in a crash.

I couldn't write Adam back alive, though I tried so hard for so long to make it work. Nothing worked to bring him back. Not blue ink. Not red ink. Not crayon. Not a permanent marker on a rock left at the crossroads between Applegate and Hillsborough.

There were grief counselors stationed at the high school for any student or community member to talk with. Jen said that I needed to go and talk to someone but she, like everyone else, thought Adam's death was just an unfortunate accident. I couldn't go and talk about my grief when I was the cause of all this. People would be talking about how much they missed him and how upset they were, and I would be focused more on me, on my guilt. Guilt that I really couldn't talk about without telling everyone my secret and what I had done.

Living here was unbearable. I needed to find a way out. I knew that I couldn't just leave. That would never fly with Jen. She'd either demand a way too detailed plan of what I'd do when I left and timely updates on my life or she'd lecture me until death and never let me go.

I had grabbed the mail on my way back from the memorial service and had just tossed it on the table. Eventually Jen would hound me for not sorting it and taking care of things instead of just leaving a heap on the kitchen table. I plopped down and pulled out all the junk mail that would find a nice new home in the recycling bin. I stacked Jen's mail in as neat of a pile that I could for her OCD. That left two pieces of mail for me. One was general issued congratulations card from the high school for graduation. Every senior got them. Mine didn't feel special and I didn't feel happy about graduating without Adam. Then there was the other envelope. I tore it open and unfolded the college admissions letter. I didn't make it into Stanford, not that I thought I would. It was more of a whim and a joke. But it gave me an idea.

Colleges I could attend due to my ability were limited. I needed to decide on a major where I couldn't rewrite history, and yet have it still be interesting. Adam and I were supposed to go together, or at least get into colleges close by to one another. Now I didn't have any location restrains except for maximum distance from Applegate. I could fake my admission into a college and leave a note for Jen saying that I got accepted early or needed to move in right away. She would probably be pissed that I left without saying goodbye, but she wouldn't think about it twice if my departure was because of that. I'd just need to pick a college and roll with it.

I could pick somewhere exciting like New York. The problem was that most of my stuff would be left behind. I could take what I needed for a week or two and then have Jen mail me the rest of my things when I got life settled. No one would know me in New York City. There'd be tons of places that I could work at and I'd be living someplace nice. I could picture finding a nice, big apartment and sharing it with someone who I might consider a friend in the future. I'd get a job doing something fun, even if it wasn't glamorous – which was something I could work up to. I could have a new normal life and I'd figure out a way to get Adam back. That would be my plan.

Jen, got accepted to Columbia University in NYC. Gotta leave today for early admission. Miss you. I'll call. – H

And there it was. Short, simple, and reassuring that I wasn't simply disappearing... even though I was planning that. Plus, I just got accepted into a really good school. They had an art program that looked interesting – from the two seconds Google search – and there was no way that I could rewrite art.

So it was settled then. I'd pack a bag and head to the bank before it closed, and before Jen got home. I'd get a bus or a train and go to the big city. My mind knew that this was the riskiest thing I've ever done and I realized that I should have planned and thought this out more. But really, I was super excited. I had never been to New York City. I'd get to see all the sites and be a tourist and have a little bit of fun. I was allowed to be a little happy. Adam would want me to be a little happy, right? Okay, maybe not so soon after killing him, but he'd want me to get out of this town. It was all he ever promised.

Chapter Three

Stepping off the Greyhound bus was the first shock. I wasn't in Massachusetts anymore. The second shock was that it was colder in New York City than it had been at home. I thought "going south" meant finding someplace warmer. Not that it really mattered now that I was already here. There was no going back for me. I pulled on my backpack and grabbed my tote bag of clothes and headed towards Time Square. Maybe it was the starry-eyed dreamer in me to go play tourist, but I was sure that going there with that enormous amount of people around would land me a new home the fastest.

The streets were a lot more crowded than Applegate, even during the huge town events like homecoming. It was strange that no one was even paying attention to me or smiling as they passed or even tried to avoid walking into me. Just because your svelte body is padded with fur, running into me while your head's down texting is not my fault. Hopefully that wasn't a sign of things to come. There had to be at least one person there looking for a roommate.

Sparkling lights, massive crowds, and delicious smells greeted me all at once in the Square. It was so much to take in. There were street carts selling nut and wieners. Laughing and smiling people looking up and everywhere. It really felt magical, like this was the place I was meant to be in and where everything that needed to happen would happen. I wanted to be like everyone else here.

I dug for my wallet in my backpack and headed to a kebab dealer. His thick accent asked me what I would like and it was hard not to tell him that I'd try one of everything. I just settled for the chicken one and watched in awe as he quickly threw it together and grilled it on the hot plate of his cart. Only after I set my money on the counter did he hand over the skewered meat. It tasted so good that I almost walked away in taste bud bliss before he could gave me back a few coins in change.

I was willing to bet that he was always here working. He probably heard some things. I was willing to bet that this guy could help me.

"Excuse me, but do you by chance know of anyone looking for a roommate? I just got to the city and need a place to stay."

He just stared at me for a moment. Surely he was more like the folks of Applegate than the prissy fur coat lady. At least he was listening to me and acknowledging that I existed. But he just shrugged his shoulders and apologized. Guess it meant that I'd have to do it the hard way. I started to walk away when someone grabbed my arm.

"Did you say you were looking for a place to stay?" A black guy, probably about five years older than me, had a hold of my arm. When I nodded my head, he let me go.

"Yea, but I don't really have that much money right now. I was hoping to find a roommate and place to live before I went looking for a job." I glanced around at all the shops and people. "I didn't think that would be too hard in a place like this."

"Nah, nah... not hard at all." He stuck his hands in the front pockets of his jeans. "But how much do you have? I got a sister looking for a roommate. Nice place. She's nice too."

I had to think about how much cash I had stuffed into my backpack before getting on the bus. Well, minus what I just paid for lunch, and I'd need a little bit for food. "Four hundred."

The guy just nodded. "That's good, good. Do you have it on you? My sister needs to pay rent today. I go give it to her and then you can move in. Sound good?"

Oh, my. His sister definitely was in a pickle then. Sounded like she was a little irresponsible, but then who was I to talk. I got Adam killed. And I did write before I left that everything would be okay. It proved to be going alright so far. I made it to New York City and now I found a place to live.

I dug out the cash and gave it to the guy. "So how does this work? I go with you and –"

"No," he cut me off. "You stay here and I'll go pay my sister. Then I come back and get you."

It seemed like a weird arrangement. There were hundreds of people here. How would he find me again? "How are you going to find me?"

He didn't hesitate. "Go stand by the Hershey store. I gotta go now."

I watched him disappear and then glanced around to find this store. I couldn't pick out the place until I looked up and saw the giant candy on the side of the building. I walked over to the corner, almost getting hit by a taxi as I crossed the street, and camped out. I'm sure it wouldn't take long.

"You can't be here." It was a voice that came from inside the store hours later.

"I'm waiting for someone. They said to meet here so they could find me."

The employee gave me a once over. Probably taking in the two bags I carried and the fact that I wasn't moving. But I was clean and presentable and clearly not some homeless person begging outside their store. What was the problem? And out of the thousands of people, how did they notice me?

"You still have to leave. It's time to move on or else we're calling the police."

That's not something that I wanted. I glanced up and down the street and noticed the bleachers. I could sit up there and wait. It was in view of the store and I'd be able to see when... god, I didn't even get his name. Why didn't I ask that, at least?

It was already starting to get cold out. Inside my backpack, there wasn't much else that I could wear over my hoodie to keep me warm. I just hoped the guy would be back soon. I just wanted to be someplace with a bed or even a couch.

The streets were clearing out slowly. With all the flashing lights, it hardly looked like night at all. A cop went out on patrol at the other end of Times Square. But still no one showed up for me. When the Hershey store closed, I went back to stand on that corner. A few people glanced my way as they walked down the street. Probably to make sure that I didn't bother them on their way to wherever they were going. Maybe it was the sound of my stomach growling that scared them away. I was too scared to leave to get something to eat because I thought that I might miss them.

I realized that I had about thirty dollars left, which should be a week's worth of food. It was enough back in Applegate. Sure the kebab cost more than I thought, but it was more like carnival food which was always special and pricier.

I had thirty dollars to my name. I was cold and hungry. I was alone.

I was screwed.

It had been a nagging thought, but now I realized what actually happened. I was scammed. I willingly handed over all my money to a stranger in a strange city where everyone was abrupt and cold. What was I thinking? The whole phone lady incident should have taught me enough to know it was stupid to hand over all my money. People in this place weren't kind like the folks of Applegate.

What could I do now? I headed towards the police hut on the other end of Times Square. A couple cops were standing outside. Maybe if I explain what happened, they could find this guy and get my money back.

"Excuse me, officer, but someone took all my money."

The taller one eyed me. "And how'd they do that?"

I didn't know that he was just humoring me. "He said he could find me a place to stay. His sister had to pay the rent right now and he needed to run off to get my money to her." It sounded even stupider to my ears now.

"So what we gonna do about it?"

I was slowly starting to see their train of thought. They assumed the same thing the store employee had. "I need you to file a report and try to find him. It was everything I have. I don't have a place to stay tonight. Please," I begged.

"We saw you working the Square all day. Why don't you just head back to the shelter with the rest of your kind for the night and leave us alone?"

Did he think I was homeless?

In Applegate, no one really turned anyone away. We looked out for each other, even though it was annoying and a pain in the ass when someone told your mom that you were out late that night or were up smoking on top of the school auditorium. The police actually helped and wanted to make things right. Clearly, I wasn't in Applegate anymore.

"Do you have a piece of paper and pen I could borrow?" I was desperate. I couldn't be out here alone at night. Where would I sleep? What would I eat? I wasn't safe.

"Get. Lost."

Not even one ray of hope.

I walked away, kind of disheartened by the injustice going on but mostly so they wouldn't see me crying. Would it make a difference if I told them I was an orphan who just graduated high school and whose boyfriend just died? I was supposed to be waiting to hear back from colleges, even Columbia right here in the city. I wasn't some random homeless person. If they knew, would it matter? ... I figured not.

I wandered these strange streets until I was thoroughly lost. I had no idea which way I came from or which way I was going. Not that it mattered. I knew nothing about this city other than somewhere there was the Statue of Liberty and there was Central Park and Broadway. Well, Broadway I had seen on my way to Times Square when I accidently took a little detour after not paying attention to the street signs. I had nothing and no one.

A shadow moved about half a block ahead of me. I froze. What was that? I could just imagine it being some mugger waiting to rob me and then would end up either laughing or killing me when they realized I had nothing left to steal.

But the shadow moved and grew closer. It walked under a store awning light and I finally saw it was just a homeless man. It was a bit of a relief, even though he was walking towards me. There was nothing to be worried about. If he asked for money, I'd explain I was broke and homeless too. He'd probably help me out or point me in the right way to get things back on track.

"Spare change?" He asked, holding out his hand.

Shaking my head, I replied, "Sorry, I have nothing. I lost all I have and I don't even have a place to stay tonight."

He glanced over my shoulder. "Seems you have more than me."

I don't know what he meant by that. I was just waiting for him to offer me some kind of help. From the state of his clothes, he clearly was out here on the streets longer than me and therefore had more experience and knowledge about this stuff. He needed to help me out, but he started to walk away.

"Please. I don't know what to do." I almost reached out and grabbed him to make him stay until he helped me.

A sigh escaped him. "There's a colony under the Brooklyn. They'll let you stick around as long as you pay the fire."

He started to walk off, leaving me with way more questions than answers. "What's the Brooklyn?" I knew there was a bridge that went over to the borough but, for all I knew, it was a street or building or company. "And what's paying the fire?"

He groaned loud enough that I heard him when he was already walking away. "The Brooklyn Bridge, girlie. And you throw something into the fire barrel. Keep everyone there warm." And with that, he hurried around the corner away from me.

But where was the Brooklyn Bridge from here? I knew where to look for street signs, but I didn't know what direction I was going in or should be walking. It was then that I realized my cell phone was in my back pocket. I had almost forgot about it. I could use it to get a map. Wait... I could use it to call the cops. If I talked to someone besides the patrol cops in Time Square, maybe someone would believe me and come to help. I was the victim of a scam, after all... a mugging, robbery, even.

There was one lone bar in the battery icon. I had forgot to charge it on the bus. There be just enough juice in the battery to either make it to the bridge or to call the cops. There wasn't going to be enough for both. Or I could call my sister, Jen, and tell her that the note I left about being accepted early to Columbia was a lie and now I lost all my money and was out on the streets. It would probably take her all night to get here, which still meant I was homeless for the night and that there was a long lecture awaiting me. But then I'd have to either tell her where I was or try to find the place she'd pick me up, and my phone would be dead and the map application would be pointless. Jen would haul me back to Applegate, and then what was the point of trying to escape? I'd be back there being pitied and questioned over Adam's death and how I was handling it. I couldn't bear to see his parents, let alone talk to them when I'd inevitably bump into them downtown.

I reached into my front pant pocket. I had enough change in there that I should be able to call Jen from a pay phone if I found one. I still could try to make it on my own. It was just go to this "colony" or call the cops. There was the risk that the cops might think the same thing as the two that were on patrol and then I'd be worse off without my phone. At least I could have a tiny clue as to where I was going. Maybe even one of the people at this colony would have some paper and a pen and I could write myself out of this... but Adam... No, he wouldn't want me to suffer like this. Never writing again was one thing, but this was a risk to my life to be on the streets. It couldn't be what he wanted for me, even if I killed him. He loved me too much to want that.

The map application took too long – for my tastes right now – to load. I forced it to search for the Brooklyn Bridge and then waited for the GPS to pick up my location. I was two miles away and it was a maze of streets to take to get there in the shortest amount of time. And with it getting close to midnight, I really wanted to make it there fast. That meant leaving my phone running while I walked the whole way, or at least got close. The streets along the way were all foreign to me.

It was a small speck of light down over the embankment on the water's edge. The map said that this was the Brooklyn Bridge, so that must be it. I wasn't sure exactly how I'd get down there but I needed to try. My phone was barely hanging on to 1% battery. Hopefully it would last long enough to let me see my way down the hill to get to the colony. I stumbled and slid at first, and then the light went out. My foot caught on something which only caused me to tumble down the hill and for the phone to go flying from my hand. There was no way I'd find it in the dark, and I could only hope to remember to get it in the morning, as long as no one else found it first.

The light was brighter the closer I got. I realized that it was from about a half dozen oil barrels that had odd stuff stuck in them to burn. One barrel burned creepily with the bottom half of – what I hoped was – a mannequin sticking out. These were homeless people. Homeless men.

I instantly felt all their eyes on me. I'm sure that I was the last thing they expected to see, and I'm sure they didn't have much of an idea of what to make of me. Although, with the way some were grabbing themselves, I could imagine how a few were thinking.

One of the older men walked over, taking in my appearance and backpack. "Can we help ya, miss?"

It was oddly the first time someone was being nice to me. "Yea, I lost all my money and have nowhere to go. I ran into a," *Was it offensive to call them homeless?* "...homeless man that told me to come to the colony and pay the fire." Well, I had said it.

"What you got in that bag?"

Okay, so maybe it wasn't offensive. I heard someone say something about me being a junker, whatever that was. Someone else snickered about a rich girl losing her daddy's money. It took everything inside me to just ignore them.

"Everything I have... just my clothes." I figured it was probably better to be safe and just play down what I had, which wasn't much more than that.

He nodded towards one of the fire barrels. "Add it to the fire."

I walked over, pulling my backpack down around one shoulder. I unzipped the top and tried to pick my least favorite thing. I couldn't burn Adam's tee or that one pair of jeans that make my ass look good. I threw in a pair of sweatpants and went to zip up my bag.

"You add more," a gruffly voice ordered from the other side of the flame. "We got nothing, so we all share 'til we all the same."

No.

"But I can't." I clutched my bag tightly and shook my head. "I got nothing."

The gruffly one stalked closer, eying my bag. My racing heartbeat was what clued me in on what was coming if I didn't toss something more into the fire. He was going to toss in my whole bag, or maybe even me. There had to be a common ground because this wasn't fair to ask of me.

"There's a guy over there with a cart full of paper and stuff." Maybe I could distract him and he'd back off.

"Junker," the man grumbled.

Again with that thing I didn't know. It seemed to be some type of person. Probably like someone being a baker or cashier. But that was going to have to be something to worry about later. I unzipped my bag enough and pulled out that favorite pair of jeans. It had been an accident. I thought my hand had closed around the other pair of jeans. It was too late to go back now.

"One more and that's it. That's more than anyone else is putting in. I just have this and my dead boyfriend's shirt, and I can't burn that."

The man stopped after I threw the denim into the flames. It seemed like at least one person cared. He grumbled, but turned back to get warm by another barrel.

I probably only had two outfits left. I had imagined that I'd find a place to live and get a job fast. I didn't imagine needing everything I did. These pants were going to have to be worn for two days in a row.

The people around the barrel – now burning with my clothes – moved a little to let me near the flames. It definitely was warmer standing there, but I was just as tired. I couldn't lay down next to it or against the hot metal thing. I didn't know if I needed sleep more or just to be warm. I could have put another layer on but I had lied about what I had and I was too scared of what they'd do if they found that out. I decided to grab a tiny grass spot – well, one without rocks – and tossed my backpack on the ground. I tried to move everything to one end so that I could almost have a pillow. I just had to pretend that I was out camping with Adam and the girls. I took a deep breath. I could do this. With the crackling sound of my clothes, it wasn't too hard to imagine a campfire with marshmallows, even if it took longer for my body to relax and fall asleep.

Something tickled, just above my hip. It stopped for a moment and I drifted more into my dreams. But then it came back, moving a little lower, and my head lolled to the side. A nagging feeling told me something wasn't right, to get up. Everything was blurry when I opened my eyes and it was all tinged orange from the fire. But gruffly man and a friend were hovering over me. One had his hands on my backpack while the other had his hand going into my pants.

I screamed, but it didn't seem to do anything other than make them stop for a moment. No one came running to step in. I needed to get out of here before they all decided they wanted something from me.

While I shoved off gruffly's friend, he grabbed my backpack and ran away with it. It was ripped open and rifled through, then tossed in the flames before I could beg him to stop. My flight instinct kicked in then and I got to my feet. I didn't know where I was going other than as far away from the colony as possible. My feet slipped as I ran back up the embankment that stole my now forgotten cellphone. I jumped over the guard rail along the road, cut across the street, and never looked back. I never stopped running.

Chapter Four

I couldn't be around the couple homeless men on the corner. No matter how much I wanted to and thought it could help. I spent a rough night alone on the streets already but it was a struggle I realized that needed to be done alone. Not to spare them, but to protect me. I had no paper or pen, but that wasn't it. I wasn't stupid enough not to realize what I am. I'm an attractive young girl, alone and desperate. Sure, I'd get their help for a night or two but they'd want something for their troubles – a trade – or maybe they'd just yank down my pants and take it one night while I'm sleeping. If only I knew they had a daughter or granddaughter my age or another female in their life that I reminded them of to gain their protection and their help.

My stomach growled.

I stepped back into the shadows and changed the route I was taking. I couldn't bet on family values and there seemed to be no other women on the streets. My odds in a group were the same as being alone. I was safer without anyone, but I was starving. So I stuck my hands in the pockets of my hoodie and went to find a clean dumpster to dig up some food. Maybe I'd strike gold and be able to write again... Then again, I deserved to be cold and miserable on the streets after what I did to Adam. But still I wondered how much more I'd have to suffer before Adam would forgive me.

There weren't many dumpsters on this block, and I knew most weren't for restaurants or grocery stores. It meant that those were pointless to dumpster dive in. Sure, I could find some torn shirt or paper or something but the probability of finding something useful was low. The only good things about those kind of dumpsters in the fashion district was that most were slightly warmer with the scraps of fabric for padding and insulation from the cold. The hazard was pins and needles being tossed in. I was debating if spending the night in one of those would be worth it. It probably would be safer than out on the street, and definitely better than things at the colony had been. I'd have a buffer against the cold and would be tucked out of sight.

My stomach growled again.

I needed to find something to eat. I didn't have the time or street reputation to be a junker. I could collect junk and try to sell it but I had no one to buy it, that and the homeless community would knock me back down to my social status in their hierarchy. That left begging on the street for change. People here had already ignored me when I was fresh off the bus, and I saw how these New Yorkers avoided the homeless. It was a whole day's job to collect just a couple dollars. It would take a week to get anything to eat. There were rumors of homeless shelters and soup kitchens, but I had yet to find out where or if I would be safe going there.

There was a couple fast food joints up on the next block. I had remembered running across them the night I sprinted away from the colony. They had smelled good enough to get me to stop, but my pride kept me from lifting the dumpster lids. Now, that pride wasn't really speaking much. I could tell that there was something rotting a little inside and it turned my stomach, but this was something I had to do. Even if it was just a few slices of tomato or a half-eaten bun, I needed to dig it out and force it down my throat.

The pungent odor hit me hard in the face when I lifted one half of the lid. I gagged and wanted to vomit. I didn't want to do this, but I had no other choice. I leaned up on my toes and reached over the edge into the dumpster, without being able to see anything. Every time my hand touched something slimy or sticky, I thought it was a monster or rat or rotten, sticky goo. Everything felt like the worst imaginable thing until I got the courage to pull something out and realized it was just a leaf of lettuce or gob of mayonnaise. But the smell this time almost turned off my starving appetite. Almost.

I needed to get closer, as much as I hated that. I stuck my foot in the slot on the side of the dumpster that the garbage truck uses to lift the container to empty it and used it to pull myself up. It looked as bad as it smelled inside. There seemed to be some half-eaten apples near the back and it looked like a loaf of bread just starting to mold... but it was in the original bag, so it was gold. The apples would need to be washed well, and that meant finding some reliably clean water in which to do that. But I could have bread again! I just needed to reach it.

Leaning out over the top, my fingers just grazed the plastic wrapping. The tip of my index finger nudged it enough that it teetered slightly closer. I leaned to get it when something moved out of the corner of my eye.

A rat!

I freaked and panicked. My foot got stuck for a moment in the slot outside and it threw me off. *It was going to eat me!* I fought to get my foot free and, when it slipped lose, I fell over the edge into the dumpster.

I fell inside.

With the rat.

That was going to eat me.

I was going to die.

I scrambled to get to my feet again and fought through the waves of trash to make it to the edge of the dumpster to pull myself back out to freedom. Nothing else mattered other than getting out. Not even the loaf of untouched bread that I crushed with my foot on my way up the dumpster wall. I flung myself out, not caring that I landed hard on my ass in freedom. Out of the side of the dumpster, I watched in horror as the same haunting rat slipped out through a rusted hole and disappeared down the alley to find darkness.

It just was so fitting. Karma would give me exactly what I want, then drive me away and toss the failure in my face. I should have just fought for what I wanted. After what I've been through, a rat really was nothing.

And now my only clothes were soaked in dumpster juice. Wherever I would go, I'd smell like a rancid piece of trash. I wouldn't be able to beg for money like this. I would starve and die. Alone. Smelling worse than death.

I just... I couldn't take this anymore. I wasn't meant to win at life, or at anything. I could just pick myself up off the ground and walk away, crying myself to death, or until I found someone to really pity me. But in this city, I wouldn't find a soul that would care.

The rustle of a shopping cart caught me off guard as I came to the end of the alley. A junker and his cart were blurry through my tears. He didn't say a word; he just pushed his cart around me. Was I so disgusting that a homeless person wouldn't even acknowledge me being alive? It was the lowest of lows. He wouldn't even offer me a scrap of fabric to wipe the sludge off my face or a couple cans to return for deposit to grab something to eat. Life was just cruel and...

He was a junker.

I used the back of my grubby hands to wipe away some of the tears. This guy had a shopping cart full of junk. I just needed a piece of paper and something to write with. Even if he had only paper, I could find something to write with. I'd sneak into a bank and used one of the pens tied down to the little table where people filled out deposit and withdrawal forms. I should be able to scribble something down before the security guard kicked my smelly ass back onto the street. I would have to risk it.

But there was no way he'd just give me a piece of paper. I'd have to steal it and hope I got away. My ass hurt from the fall out of the dumpster and I wasn't sure I'd be able to run away fast enough. I was willing to bet that he wouldn't call out for the cops or for someone to stop me over a piece of paper. Who'd help a homeless person? Even if he chose to run after me, he'd either have to leave his whole treasure to grab me or run after me with the wobbly shopping cart. I could probably outrun him with the cart.

I started to follow behind him, waiting for a chance. I wouldn't have time to look for a pen in the cart but I could see where the stack of papers were, and there weren't many. I'd only have one shot at this. I waited until he stopped and turned his back to dig into a smaller street corner trash can. Then I ran pass him, my legs and hips and ass aching and shooting out pain. He didn't seemed to notice me until I bumped into his cart and got caught with my hand in it.

"Get the fuck gone!" He yelled, turning back to grab me.

My hand was already on his whole stack of used receipts, old flyers, and crumbled newspaper. I was stepping out into the street when he ran around his cart. I was in the middle of the street, dodging traffic because I crossed on a red pedestrian light, when his cursing and yelling got louder. I didn't look back once I made it to the other side. I kept limping and running until I was a couple blocks away. There hadn't been any wonky metal wheel sounds chasing me, and behind me there was no sight of the homeless junker. I had gotten away, and gotten lost. Again.

I was out of breath and now in need of a bank. But first, I needed to look at my score and figure out what I could use. The newspaper was soggy and unusable. The receipts were too small to write out much, and I needed to be exact and wordy to write everything I needed right now. Those got trashed, again, as I turned over the flyers in my hand. The back of a few were blank and had enough space to write, but there were only two that I could do anything with. That meant I only had two chances to get everything right. It was a lot of pressure when I thought about how screwed I was if I had to stay on the street another night.

Shoving the two pieces of workable paper into my pocket, I walked the streets with my eyes open for a bank or anything with a pen. I passed food vendors and tourists that parted the sidewalk to avoid me, like Moses parting the sea. I wouldn't be allowed close enough to humanity to be able to find and use a pen. I took a seat on the curb and tried to figure out my options. I could try to rob someone and hope they had a pen on them. I could scour the streets for a writing utensil that had been dropped and forgotten. Or I would find a way to use myself. I don't think I'd be above writing words out from my own shit at this point... or I could use my blood. I could find something to poke my finger and just write. I knew where the latter two would work.

I headed into Central Park and looked for any rose bushes with thorns or any small twigs that I could use to prick myself. I managed to find a small twig and a spot away from people. Against the concrete walkway, I rubbed one end of the twig into a sharp point. I didn't want to watch, but I had to just in case this was my only shot – either the twig could miss and break or I'd chicken out stabbing myself a second time. I brought it down

49

hard on the back of my hand. It sank into my skin and it throbbed long after I pulled it out. The tip of the twig was bloody enough that I could scratch out something. So I set a piece of paper out on my lap and used my blood to write me somewhere better. Each time I stuck the twig into my wound, I flinched and cried a little more from the pain.

Haley Brown is accepted to Columbia University on full scholarship and moves into the dorms today. No one notices her smell or looks. New clothes are in the dorm room for her. $100 are in the pocket of her jeans. A car is driving to Central Park to pick her up in 5 min. No one remembers her being on the streets.

Chapter Five

"Haven't you ever used your powers to get something you wanted? I don't believe you've always used them for good or kept it hidden. Nobody is that good of a liar to keep something like this quiet."

My best friend did have a point. This thing of mine was too big of a secret to keep forever... even I knew that. The best I had been able to do was keep quiet about it and hope nobody found out. It wasn't like people really knew me before I came to New York City, and people here just didn't care. It was something I never really had to work hard to protect. That was until she stumbled onto my weird ramblings in my journal and thought I was just scribbling down the news audio bytes. Well, until Meghan saw one I wrote before it happened. Awfully hard to come up with an alibi for that.

And I did use my power for something I wanted once... He still haunts me.

"I'm not perfect."

Rolling my eyes, I took a sip of my Starbucks. It was basically the only reason I got out of bed. Well, I guess going to class so I don't fail and can graduate in the spring was a good motivator. But coffee...

"Haley," she huffed out my name. She so was not giving this up, and she probably was getting to her limit with me. It wasn't like I purposely tried to be difficult all the time. It was just that she kept pushing me to use these powers. Booty calls, needing to squeeze into skinny jeans, and making her pass an exam weren't exactly reasons I should be writing. I purposely avoided a college major where there was a lot of writing involved. Who knew what I'd spawn out into the world? But that's just what she wanted me to do for her. It was mid-term season, after all.

"Just a little help with the composition exam. You know Professor Helfrich fails everyone their first year just so he can make twice the amount of money by getting us next year for a redo of his pointless class."

Yea, I'm so sure the cranky old man had that evil master plan. I had to sit through the required class. It *was* horrible, but it was doable. Sure I scrapped by with a C- which destroyed my overall GPA and probably nix my future chances at an awesome career, but the important thing was that it was done and over with and could be blocked from my memory forever.

Shaking my head at her begging definitely wasn't the answer Meghan wanted. If she hadn't grabbed her cup of coffee, another scoff or huff or snipe might have come from her. "It's not like anything bad ever happened 'cos of it."

And there it was. The crossroads. Literally and figuratively. Adam.

"Someone I cared a lot for died," I mumbled into my coffee.

There. Let her take in that and think about it. Someone died. My powers were real and horrible. I could have just said nothing. I probably should have just said nothing. Meghan probably wouldn't believe me until I started saying names and details, and then she'd only believe me after she looked it up on her phone. I shouldn't have brought it up and avoided mentioning it like every other time she tried to guilt me in to something. Although, part of me hoped that this might actually stop her from so casually asking and thinking I wasn't just being a bitch for holding out on her. Maybe...

"Yea, Haley, like I believe that." Meghan sounded oddly mad. "I didn't think you'd actually try to be so low as to lie about something like that. Just tell me no and that it's not going to happen. Geez... I thought we were better friends than that."

Oh-kay. So she thought I was lying to her. Maybe I should just roll with it. After all, it was what she apparently believed. Why burst that bubble and going through all the hassle of trying to explain to get it through her head that I wasn't lying to her. Not to mention all the emotional baggage it was surely going to bring up. Letting Meghan think I put little faith in her and was just lying seemed like a fair enough price for my secret. Then again, I kind of did need her to like me. She was one of my only friends but, more importantly, Meghan was my roommate. I wasn't going through hell again to try and find someone I wouldn't jump at the chance to kill, maim, or make wander into the bakery downtown to get a sugar rush and have that rush crash her on the couch of Delta Omega. In all fairness, that last roommate ended up getting one hot boyfriend out of it.

Sighing, I knew there was no way out but to spill. "His name was Adam Montgomery. He was my high school boyfriend and I loved him." At least the anger on her face dialed back a notch. Even if it was a teeny tiny notch. "I used to write a lot back then and he was the only person that knew everything. Well, besides Jen. But even though he knew what I could do for him, Adam never wanted me to write about him. I don't really know why. Maybe he was scared that I'd slip in something else to make him do stuff for me or whatever, but he had wanted to be in control of his own life and his own future."

I had to take a break and force myself to take a sip of my coffee. "I always wondered why he never asked for my help," I mused into the dark liquid. "You know, maybe he was just saving it up for one huge favor. It sure seemed to have turned out like that at the end."

Something touched my hand and I jumped, trying to calm my brain fast enough that I didn't spill my boiling hot coffee all down the front of my body. Then I'd have the horrible burns to match the horrible curse. It would be almost melancholic fate. It was the way Adam had gone out. But the cause of my accident would have been Meghan. I had been so focused in my own little world that I didn't see her hand reaching out to comfort me, nor did I realize that all anger was gone from her face and replaced by concern and something else that I didn't have the focus to really think about right now.

My face cracked a small smile. It was a little nice to be comforted, even though I was the villain in this story. I could have stopped it all if I hadn't been so selfish. Maybe being selfish in the past would save Meghan in the present.

"It was just before graduation when he asked if I could make him a writer like me." It seemed so nonchalant to say it that way. That's what I was and only hid what I was in plain sight, but it still left a bad feeling in my body. "There was a car crash which had triggered me when I was a kid. My parents ended up dying because of it. I was in a coma and then had years of fun between therapists and recovering and struggling to get by with Jen and what family still cared about me. I didn't want all that to happen to Adam, so I took all night and thought it all out. I tried to put every safeguard and detail in the right place. He was only supposed to hit a telephone pole, get a small bump on his head, be in a coma for a week, then be back at home and writing with me. We were going to graduate and get married. He was the one... the only one."

My throat felt like it was closing up. "He still is," my broken voice admitted.

Meghan got up and dragged her chair around next to me. I knew what she was thinking. Helping her cheat on an exam score wasn't going to put her life in danger. It was minute compared to that. I bet she wanted to console me and say that the same wouldn't happen to her and that it was a one-time thing.

"Haley, I'm so sorry. I didn't know." How could she have known? "I get why you don't date or go to any of the big frat parties. What happened to Adam isn't your fault."

That caused me to pull back and look at her. How could she say that? How could she say that it wasn't my fault after I admitted to writing about Adam? How could she say that when she knew how I made things happen and how it always happened exactly how I wrote them?

"That's bullshit, Meg." I stood up, my legs pushing back my chair.

She reached for my hand as I tried to move around the table. For now, she succeeded in stopping me.

"Come on, Haley. Don't just run away. You're beating yourself up over something you shouldn't be holding yourself responsibly for." She got up as well. That comment about running away got to me, but not as much as the idea of her following me. I just needed some space. I needed to get away from people... People that I realized were now staring at us. With or without her, I needed to get out of here.

I threw the half drank cup of coffee in the trash on the way. The inevitable caffeine crash that would come later would just be something I dealt with. There was no way I was scrounging up enough coins out of the couch to buy another cup. That and there was no way I was walking back into that store today. People would remember me and Halloween was too far in the past for wigs to be readily available to disguise my appearance. A black hoodie, baseball cap, and sunglasses might scream out that I'm robbing the place instead of getting a much needed shot of life.

"Haley, will you just wait up?"

Meghan came out of the store, letting the door bang behind her, and hurried to catch up to me. It was just my luck that the walk light was red and traffic was a tad too heavy to risk my life crossing the street. Sure, it was New York City and that's the way people were. But my mind wasn't sharp and focused at the moment from being in the deep end of a swimming pool of emotions. I couldn't write myself alive if I was dead. I had no choice but to let Meghan catch up... and talk to her. Well, let her talk to me.

"I get how you think this is your fault, but let me tell you something. He asked you. He could have told you what to write or done it himself and just let you copy it down. But he didn't do that, right?"

She stepped in front of me just as the walk light turned green. The New Yorker in me now wanted to just push her to the side and continue on my way to self-loathing and probably some bad decisions. Against my better judgement, I stayed put and let the walk sign turn red again.

Shaking my head, I let her know how much I didn't believe her weak attempts to make my life all roses and sunshine again. "You want me to blame a dead guy..." I couldn't believe that's honestly what she was asking me to do.

"No, Haley. I want you to see that it wasn't all your fault. You're still hanging onto all this guilt and it's eating you up. And you're taking it out on me."

That was it. I wasn't going to have her guilt me into cheating for her. I was not taking it out on her. If I couldn't cross the street this way, I'd cross now and walk on the other side, going the same way I wanted.

She wasn't giving up. Meghan started following me until I stopped in the middle of the street.

"Fuck off, Meg. Okay? I wasn't taking this out on you but now you're making me."

A car horn told me to move along and I grumbled all the way to the safety of the sidewalk. Maybe humanity needed a nice break from the modern world... and their cars. Seriously. This was New York City. It was pretty much pointless to have a car here when it took you an hour to go a block. Nooo... subways, buses, and taxis were too inconvenient!

Okay, now I was in a pissy mood. I had Cheerios for breakfast and now someone had pissed in them.

But when I turned around after getting to the sidewalk, she wasn't there. It was like Meghan was erased from the face of the earth without a single trace. If I didn't know any better, I would have thought I had done it.

I also knew that at some point I needed to face Meghan again. I knew that I probably owed her an apology. I knew that I needed to make amends with probably the only real friend I had. She was definitely the only one that knew the real me. I also knew that before I did that, I needed to get out a good cry and eat a tub of blue moon flavored ice cream. Being reminded of Adam, again, was worse than any break-up anyone has ever went through. That much I was sure of.

I had done my wallowing. I had my pity party. Now I needed to beg and grovel.

Where was Meghan?

She couldn't be that pissed off at me still. I knew I gave her a guilt trip and then turned bitchy. We had arguments in the past. There really was nothing that ever kept us apart. We were girls and we both knew we had our bitchy moments but we still loved each other.

I was wearing a hole in the floor from my pacing, but it couldn't be helped. Her last class of the day was over hours ago and I had a couple hot pizzas sitting on the counter in the kitchen as a peace offering. They were from Meghan's favorite place too. Even though I detested pineapple on a pizza, I felt that much guilt and regret over earlier and ordered her two. Well, one and a half. A girl still needed to eat. Luckily the pizza guy was nice enough to keep the pineapple far away from my half with pepperoni.

The thing that bothered me was that this was so unlike Meghan. She kept to a schedule, and I doubted that because of our spat earlier that she'd really avoid me. She knew me well enough to know that I probably cooled off and was feeling incredibly guilty – the perfect time to lecture me and guilt trip me into doing something more.

Me: *Where u at?*

I send the text and waited. The little icon next to the message didn't turn green. That meant her phone must be off. So that ruled out calling and begging her forgiveness... and possibly having to bribe her with the pizza just to get her home. I felt uneasy when we were at odds, especially with her being a bit MIA at the moment.

Every girl tingly sense was, well, tingling and telling me to blow up her phone with text messages. I just knew that they'd do no good. If she didn't get my first text then... oh. The little icon next to the text bubble was green now. It switched to red before my eyes. Meghan got my text, and read my text. Now where were the little speech bubble with the dots to tell me that she was writing a reply?

Come on, Meghan.

The speech bubble disappeared. She couldn't really be *that* mad at me. I mean, she could, but this was Meghan... and she was texting me back! Wait, no she wasn't. The little dots stopped... No, she was texting me! ... This bitch was toying with my emotions and I just wasn't going to have it. Fine. If that's how she wanted to play this then I was grabbing my half of the pizza and going to my bedroom.

I reached up into the cupboards to grab a plate, seeing as I wasn't going to continue pacing and make another pass by the pizza empty handed. It clanked down on the counter while I popped open the cardboard box lid. Three slices got tossed onto the plate and the last one just hung from my mouth. What? I was hungry. The plate of deliciousness was in my hands as I walked towards my room... and heard my phone beep with a text message.

Groaning, I kicked open my door and set the plate down on top of the plaid comforter on my bed. If I was going to be emotionally knocked around today, I might as well be completely lazy and eat in bed with a marathon of the Golden Girls – a terrible guilty pleasure I acquired in middle school.

I pulled the phone from my back pocket and almost dropped it when I saw what was on the lock screen. It was just a couple lines, but it sent a shiver down my spine.

Meghan: We know who you are now. We killed your friend. You are next.

It couldn't be true. Meghan must have forgot her phone at some frat house she swung by. Yea, that was it. She just needed a drink and some overly eager guy to flirt her back into a good mood. It probably was healthier than the alternative of binging on pork rinds and ice cream. She probably was just messing with me.

Me: Not funny Meg. Cut da shit and call.

Maybe whoever was playing this game – either because she asked them or because she had a blonde moment – would give up the jig now that it seemed like I caught on and wasn't going to just play along.

And now the phone was ringing. I knew it was some fucked up prank. She was probably sitting outside the building just waiting for me to freak out.

"Haley Brown. Thank you for answering and thank you to your friend for having your picture identify your contact information."

Okay, I was freaking out now. Just who the hell was this creep ass guy? First he claims they killed Meghan and now they were all kinds of creepy stalker.

"We've been trying so hard to find you. You have two choices. One, you agree to become part of us and do as we order –"

"Why the hell would I want to do that?" Sounded an awful lot like being this guy's slave and I just wasn't down for that. He definitely was a creeper after admitting to have been trying to find me, and maybe even watching me too.

The man on the other end of the phone call laughed. He laughed and it made me feel sick. Not that pervert kind of sick when you found out your privacy was invaded. It was that sick kind of feeling where you knew something bad was going to happen. Something worse than bad was what was waiting.

"Because, Haley, we know who you are now. We know where to find you and we know you wouldn't want everyone you've ever known to be killed one by one. That would be on your conscience. Is that something you could live with?"

Hell, no.

It wasn't something I think anyone could live with, but that didn't give me much options. It gave me one other, in fact. Either people died or I did whatever they wanted. And if they killed Meghan, well, I doubted doing as they said wouldn't keep people alive. But was it better to keep people I knew alive or know that I never killed anyone.

Well, that was a lie.

I had killed Adam. I was already a killer. Why not try to keep *someone* alive, even if it meant someone else would pay the price.

"W-what would I have to do?"

A gunshot pierced my eardrum through the phone. What the hell was all that about? Was the guy just a dick?

"That was one of your professors, Haley. You really should learn not to ask questions."

He laughed. I believed him though. If they had Meghan's phone and said she was dead – and had a gun! – then I couldn't see why they didn't grab one of my professors. Chances were that it was one of Meghan's but we did have a couple that we shared, just at different times. They must have grabbed her and the professor from her last class. Even if it wasn't really *my* professor, it was still another notch in my belt as far as body counts went and I didn't want there to be any, especially after Adam.

I didn't say a word. Then again, neither did he. I had to pull the phone away from my head to check that we were still on the line with each other. It was torturous not to say a word. Well, torturous was listening to someone die. Well, at least a gunshot that probably – allegedly – killed someone. Either way, it was a poor choice of words, I guess. But what this was, it had to be a test. I hated them thinking that I was nothing more than a trained poodle right now. It just didn't feel right and I knew that I couldn't be that. Not for long. As soon as I got off the phone, I'd have to write. I'd have to get out of this and see if somehow I could make things different and save Meghan. She wanted me to write about her, but I bet she never imagined it would have been like this.

The problem was that I had no clue how they found me out. I doubted Meghan ran off and told the big bad guys in their big bad guy lair... even if that was a thing. No one from my hometown, besides Jen, knew or even could take a wild guess at what I could do. Sure, I had occasionally used it for myself even though I let Meghan believe I was a saint and genius while she failed the same assignments or test. But even then, there was no way to prove what I had done and it would only be a professor that could figure it out. Besides, I always made it out to be kind of a whim that they would suddenly wish to grant me a higher grade than I deserved. The only thing that I could think of was that someone overheard me or us.

Seeing as it just bit me in the ass today, maybe it was someone from the coffee shop. Meghan had made a scene and almost the whole place had turned their attention onto us. Maybe someone was close enough to hear our bickering and was clued in. If they really were looking for me as long as they claimed, then hearing about some ability and writing and then about Adam's death probably drew a huge target on my back. They could have gotten up after Meghan left and followed us out. That wasn't a crazy kind of concept – people were allowed to leave when they were finished with their drink or eating their pastry or whatever. Whoever it was could have also been lurking around a corner listening to us and watching me leave. If I was on the other side of the street but Meghan ended up right next to them, of course they'd think to grab her and get to me through her. They had my name and knew people I cared about.

The problem was just how I fix that.

I didn't have a name. I didn't have anything to identify them. I knew nothing about this person to put any detail into rewriting what happened. The best option I had was to make everyone in that Starbucks die, which was something I absolutely didn't want to do. Even though I hated this secret, it already cost two more lives. There were tons of innocent people in that packed place today. Tons of innocent people that might not have done anything wrong except crave a caffeine boost at the same time I strolled in and grabbed my own cup of coffee. And, if I did that, I could end up killing way more people than whatever this creepy asshole stranger on the other end of the phone wanted. They could want money or an identity change for all I knew... even if they were technically a murderer and statistically probably wanted me to be the one to do all the dirty work remotely with no possible connection to me or him or whatever group I was trying to be sucked into.

The only option was to rewrite what happened this morning. I needed to remember exactly what we both did leading up to going to Starbucks. I remember that I grabbed my stuff and hit the shower. I got out, got dressed, and then looked for Meghan. And Meghan... shit! She had left sometime while I was in the shower and had texted me that she'd meet me at Starbucks before going to class. I had no idea what she had done today and there was no way that I could ask her.

I could just rewrite her whole morning. It would suck incredibly if there was stuff she actually had to do, like turn in an assignment or some kind of registration for her clubs or get something or graduation or for whatever else it was that she did in her free time. Hell, I might even get her killed if she had gone to some doctor's appointment and been given the cure for that one thing or another that was doing that one thing that... Okay, well, I was pretty sure Meghan wasn't terminally ill or even had a stuffy nose. I'm just going to file that insane panic attack in the pile of pointless stuff I could think about while not on the phone with a killer.

"Leave your apartment and go to your mailbox. Follow it precisely."

This creep was watching me.

I didn't move. His voice had knocked me out of my thoughts and I remembered what a twisted and sick mess I was currently standing in.

"Go now, Haley Brown," he ordered.

Shit! He really was watching me. He could see me right now too!

I instinctively glanced at the windows. The curtains were closed there. I knew outside my front door that there was a windowless portion of the wall across the hall from it. There was no way this guy could see me unless he was downstairs and out front watching the mailboxes or he... Could he really have gotten inside my apartment and hid cameras? It was too creepy to think about. I needed to solve that problem first and fast. Who knew what he already saw and what he was already going to use against me?

My feet slowly moved in front of each other to the point where I got to the front door. My hand, shakenly, took my set of house keys off the hook on the wall and shoved them in my pocket.

"Good girl, Haley Brown."

Yea, this fucking creep had something in my apartment to watch me. It meant I probably couldn't write here without getting caught and then there was a possibility of being stopped. I had to grab what this guy wanted and get out of here. The only thing was that there really wasn't anywhere safe anymore. The thing working on my side was that they seemed to have just found out who I was and couldn't possibly know my routine. They wouldn't know how strange it would be for me to leave now and go to, say, the library or some frat house. Yea, the latter was tricky, but blocking a bunch of drunk people out of a room for ten minutes was going to be a walk in the park compared to figuring out if there were any blind spots in my apartment and how long I had until this insane murderer busted through my door and... well, probably murdered me or at least chopped off my hands to stop me from writing. Wait. Then what would the point be in forcing me to do their dirty work? Guess there wouldn't be. Yea, I'd be dead – literally – if I tried writing here.

I grabbed my backpack off the ground and slipped my feet into my shoes. Coming back up to the apartment to leave right after getting this thing might be sending a red flag and I might be able to pull this off if I just avoided doing that. If it was as bad as I thought it was, then I only had one shot at this. If I got this wrong, then it wasn't just letting down Meghan and not saving her... it was letting down myself and losing my life. Maybe. Probably.

It was kind of pointless, given that someone already invaded my home, but I locked the front door on the way out. The hallway was quiet as I made my way to the stairs. That wasn't anything too strange. It was getting close to finals and graduation and everyone was in cram mode. That or out at one of the fraternity houses downing their body weight in alcohol to forget their woes. Hell, what I wouldn't give to be doing just that. Although, I doubted the woes of tonight would allow me to drown them out, let alone forget for an hour or so.

The mailboxes were right next to the large windows of the apartment building lobby. I was going to be watched very closely. I had just the single flight of stairs to make sure my emotions were in check and that none of my panic and fear were written on my face. Although, I just found out my best friend and roommate was dead and then heard someone else get shot. I think I could be a little rattled. But I couldn't have my escape plan on my face. Guess I should be looking shocked instead of like I had somewhere I wanted to go and any kind of determination on my face. I needed to be a shell of a person running on auto-pilot.

My foot hit the last step and it was game on. I focused on walking over to the rows of mailboxes and stuck my key in the third hole. It seemed strange that there was something in there, even though the creepy man voice said there would be something waiting. It didn't make sense because the only way to load these were from the back office. Either they picked the lock on my mailbox door, stole Meghan's key off her body – wow, that sounded calloused in my head – or they somehow got into the back room or had someone on the inside. That sounded stupid. This wasn't a bank heist. There was no "inside man".

This was my life.

And it was fucked up.

I stuck my hand into the metal tomb and pulled out the envelope. My hands were shaking – actually shaking – as I pulled the folded over part from the back and reached for the sliver of paper inside. The now empty envelope was put back into the mailbox. Staring down at the single piece of paper, I unfolded it, and slightly marveled at how anal this person must be to have folded it perfectly into thirds and made it fit like a glove in the envelope. There was blank print all the way down one side of the page.

There were no numbers on this hit list. Just a long list of names. It could mean anything. Maybe I just needed to meet these people or verbally warn them to stay off the lawn or to stop littering. Unfortunately, I doubted anyone would go to this measure if it was just about trash or annoying behaviors. Asking the creepy man outright was simply out of the question. The professor was proof of that.

Every single person had to be murdered.

They might as well have shot me. My body was numb. It felt like all the blood was gone from my body as my eyes drifted down the list. It seemed to never end. How was killing all these people going to be the lesser evil than letting people I knew die? It wasn't. There was only one person left alive that I cared about and she wasn't anywhere near campus. I didn't know if Jen was even going to be able to come see me graduate at all or if she was working the night shift again.

I tried to rationalize the predicament out. All these people on this list were probably going to die with or without me involved. This murderer might know my name now but he didn't know that, after killing Meghan, there was no one to play hostage in this game. Sure I knew people in class or those that served me my coffee but – if I was being completely honest with myself – I'm not sure I'd save them over anyone else. That would be like taking a bullet for a stranger I never met and never even spoke to before. It was ridiculous.

I pulled my backpack around my body and yanked open the zipper far enough to shove the list inside. Only the first ten names really blurred together in my mind, but I wasn't sure I wanted to see the other half of the list. If I could sit down somewhere and write then none of it would matter anyways. They'd never find me. I'd never be the reason anyone else was dead.

God, I felt like I was going to hurl.

Backpack on, head down, I headed out of my apartment building. The squares of the sidewalk disappeared just as fast as they appeared as I hurried along campus. I needed to get to the library. I could disappear in the stack of books. I could just sit and think. My phone rang from my backpack where I had tossed it at the last minute, but I was too oblivious to register that someone was trying to get ahold of me. Even if I had, I wouldn't want to talk to anyone at the moment. How could the little moments of life still exist and go on when someone had just died tonight? How could I laugh and make small talk?

It was impossible.

I didn't stop or slow down once on the mile and a half walk to the library. Not until I was a block away and the walk light turned red a second too soon. I could have chanced it with the whole five cars out on the road but, having to take a pause in my plan, my nerves couldn't handle anything else. The severity and magnitude of it was actually starting to hit me. I couldn't do this.

I couldn't do this.

I couldn't –

I screamed as someone grabbed my arm. They turned me around to face their bulky self. Dressed in all black, I should have been worried they were going to mug me or drag me to some alley and rape me. It wasn't like that had ever happened on campus, but this was still the city.

And now they had their hand over my mouth to silence me. There didn't seem to be another living creature around, or none that seemed to want to help me. My blood was pumping so hard that I could hear it in my ears and feel it in my toes.

I was going to die after all. I couldn't stop it, just like I couldn't stop Adam or Meghan from dying. I sucked. I really, really sucked. I was going to die and the thought terrified me. Cold beads of fear ran down my face and off my cheek. And they didn't stop. I knew I could beg for my life, but I also knew there was no point. I knew who this towering man had to be and I knew what he had already done tonight. When he laughed at my sniffling and tears and how my body shook from the fear, I knew everything I fear was true.

I was going to die.

"Remember right now, Haley Brown," he whispered in my ear after leaning in closer to me. "This fear. This pain."

The sickness rose in up in my stomach as my skin prickled beneath the touch of his lips as they dragged across my cheek and down towards my throat. He kissed my neck just below my ear and it tore me in two. My body had wished for someone to hold me close and be intimate like that. Like Adam. I wanted the caresses and nibbles on my neck. But my mind knew full well what was going on and who was toying with me at this dangerous moment. That was someone that I didn't want touching me. At all. I had to force myself not to fight the way he was holding me or the way his mouth was moving along the edge of my vee-necked tee. I needed to get of this alive.

"Make them suffer."

And just like that, his tender touch was gone.

His hands shoved me back so hard that I fell backwards and laid sprawled out on the concrete. It was like I was an offensive, unwanted piece of trash. I didn't know whether to argue and fight – which made it seem like I had wanted him to touch and use my body – or to be relieved I was a couple feet away, even though I had the disadvantage of being off my feet and scrapped up.

He turned around and walked to the corner before disappearing around the edge of building. It felt surreal. Not only the whole encounter and what lead up to it, but also the fact that as a grown woman I was so terrified of dying that I soiled myself.

The crotch of my jeans was soaked and my body wouldn't stop shaking. And it wasn't from the slight chill in the air from the night. The wetness made the material stick to me and froze my skin just below it. Walking into the library now would only leave me embarrassed. I'd never be able to face anyone ever again. On the other hand, I'd either be dead or a murderer and not allowed out in public. I'd never see any other those people again.

My mind wasn't even throwing out the idea that I could write myself out of their eyesight. Guess shock and fear can made you kind of oblivious to everything else. Oblivious to the gasps then snickers and giggles as I walked into the library. Oblivious to the hushed comments and jokes as I walked towards the back to the reference section – one place that was guaranteed to be void of a living soul. And there, in the furthest corner from humanity, was a chair and that was where I planted myself. All that greeted me was the sound of silence.

That made me break.

The tears were flowing again as the realization that I was really alone hit. Not just at this moment, but basically in my whole life. I had only one family member left but she was busy with her life, and I didn't want to count Jen while I was having my pity party. I never dated anyone. I didn't have any other friends. Now I was sitting in the campus library, pants piss-soaked, and scared shitless over this huge decision in front of me that some hulking creeper forced me into.

I smeared the moisture from my eyes and dug in my backpack for that list. If nothing else, it was just a source of paper. In the least, it looked like I was going to write them out of existence if tall, dark and murderous was still hanging around and watching me through the bookcases.

What proved to be the hard part, oddly, was finding a pen or pencil. The tears were manageable and I knew that there was no way I was going to be weak enough to let them stop me. I was *The Writer*. I could fix this. I was the only one that could and I had to.

I laid down the paper and flattened it out with the palm of my hand. It seemed the backpack had added quite a few more creases and folds. And then I added a few drops of tears from my face as I froze over it, my eyes frozen dead on one name.

Jennifer Ann Garrison

It couldn't be just a coincidence. That was my sister. Not just that, but they found her by her married name. Either that creep knew who I was longer than he let on or he was really good at digging up my life. All the more reason to hurry.

Flipping over the paper, I started to make a list of the things I knew that needed to be changed: *where Meghan went this morning; where we met and what we talked about; what needed to happen after we left.*

It seemed like that was all, but it didn't feel right. It should change things enough to save Meghan and maybe stop the connection between The Writer and me from being made. But there was always the risk that my secret wasn't found out that way. I only had one shot to write and get this right.

Meghan and Jen were the two people that were going to be ripped out of my life. I couldn't save them both. At least not right now. Well, not anymore now that Meghan was dead and Jen was on the list that I had hoped would save her if I agreed to this madness. There was only one way to keep Jen's name off this list. If I did what had to be done, it would probably kill me inside. But if the other things on the list solved my problem then I could afford to be a little selfish. I picked up my pen again and added one more thing to my list.

Everyone but Jen will forget that we're related and that we know each other.

It would be the safest way to keep her safe. I'd still have my sister, in some small way. After I wrote this out and calmed down a bit, I'd have to call her and explain. But that was it. How could I explain something she'd see as the future when it would have happened already in our past? I could try to explain that it was like an alternate dimension kind of thing and that she couldn't start telling other people about me. I wasn't sure I would be able to explain this one to her or if she'd understand why it had to come down to this. I was supposed to be the all-powerful one, as she put it. The nagging thought was over me wondering if this – I – wouldn't just be another burden on her. I could make Jen forget all about me and maybe she'd be happier for that. I would lose everything once today and again tomorrow.

No, I think I have to completely let go. I would have Meghan, but I couldn't have my sister. It would be too hard to keep the lies and stories straight. After I wrote what I needed to in order to make it to morning alive, I'd write the last item I was adding to my list:

Jen Ann Garrison lost her parents and her unborn baby sister. She always wished she knew her and imagined that she was a big sister as a kid. The caring, over-protective big sister attitude stuck with her. Haley Brown not exist to people in Applegate or who knew her before college.

But after making that way too detailed note, my brain realized what happened a moment too late. I wrote it. It was already done. For the second time tonight, I stared at words that were life changing and had changed my whole life. This really did mean I had no one but Meghan now.

I was numb. I was dumb.

Maybe it was the bliss of ignorance from all the shock or my brain finally fried and I would never care about anything ever again. I had lost my sister – a person that would never know who I am or that I ever existed outside her own imagination. Imagination that made this horrible thing possible. And I hadn't even thought to write it out better for her. Who knew what side effects my half-baked words just cost her. Words that I couldn't rewrite and change.

I should have known better. I should have known that any word written from my hand had to be vague, open-ended, and just words without complete functioning sentences. Jen had always been the one to push me to set limits and constantly reminded me of my rules and the consequences. Seemed apt that she was written out of my life the first time I forgot that.

I deserved to lose her.

Did I even deserve to have Meghan back?

If I could so carelessly throw away my own sister, what chance did my best friend have? Sure, Meghan knew everything about me and had gotten much closer to who I was as a person than my real sister. To be honest, Meghan was like a sister to me. My real family, and then the one I ended up choosing. But this wasn't all about me. Meghan had a family that loved her. She had a full life ahead of her that was more than worth living for. She was talented and kind and funny and going places. She deserved to live, and I couldn't just walk away from my problems now that there wasn't anyone else to fight for. I had to go back and fight for her yesterday and this morning and a few hours ago.

I needed to bring her back in a way that I couldn't bring Adam back. His death had been at the reckoning of my pen, but Meghan's wasn't. Maybe it meant that there was still a chance for her. If there was honestly nothing that I could do, then I would just leave. I'd leave this life and let the chips fall as they may. I'd protect the rest of the world from knowing me and getting involved. I just had to try to make one more difference in the world first.

It was a risk, but I flipped the paper over to look at the long list of names. For once, since this whole thing started, I was relieved. Jen's name was no longer on the list. Someone else's name had replaced hers. Someone I didn't know. Someone I'd never know.

With that boost of confidence and reassurance, I turned the sheet of paper back over and adjusted the grip of the pen in my hand. Taking a deep breath, I mentally started piecing the words that needed to be say together in my head. I needed this to be right, without any doubt.

This morning Meghan Galloway woke up late and got out of bed at eleven o'clock. If she heard the shower running, she knew it was her roommate and decided to wait around for her. Meghan got dressed casually and wanted to suggest to Haley that they get lunch at the Campus Café instead of grabbing coffee at Starbucks. Haley grumbles about her caffeine needs but gives in. They place their orders and find a table mostly away from other people. Meghan does not bring up the fact that Haley is The Writer and does not ask for written help in her schoolwork and exams. No one overhears what they talk about. They both get up and leave on friendly terms. Meghan makes it to class five minutes early. She attends class and makes it home safely where her roommate has Pizzario's Pizza waiting and the Golden Girls set on the DVR.

I took a moment to read over it one last time, even though the past was already in the process of rewriting itself. I could feel some changes affecting my body already. I felt more tired and knew there hadn't been a strong shot of caffeine running through my veins because Starbucks never happened. I could feel a bit happier over my morning and afternoon when I thought of Meghan. That must have meant we didn't fight and get into a huge argument. She mustn't have asked me to write about her. And the pizza... I could still smell the pineapple sacrilege in my thoughts. I just couldn't tell if I had saved my best friend.

I reached down to the backpack between my feet to pull out my cell phone. I should have written away pissing my pants, but that was neither here nor there. It was so minor compared to everything else. I unlocked the screen on my phone and plugged in her phone number. Holding it to my ear, I could hear it ringing. And ringing... and ringing.

Why wasn't she picking up?

I knew Meghan wasn't mad at me, because I purposely wrote that away. And I didn't have had the chance to screw things up again. She must have jumped in the shower or something. That's probably what she did. She had a long day at class or something. I mean, I felt happier about this morning and I obviously had pizza. Even with piss-soaked pants, I was happy. I just needed to walk home and find my proof.

My reputation and self-esteem took a serious hit though as I walked back through the lobby to the front door. The same people that had snickered and laughed at me had immediately spotted my return and had new, louder, ammunition. This time they actually wanted me to hear them. But I didn't care. I had just raised someone from the dead.

The outside world was what had me more worried. Stepping out of what I considered the safety zone amongst the books, the hair on my spine stood on end. It felt like there was someone still watching me as I headed along the dimly light street back towards the apartment. It was impossible to shake the idea that someone was going to reach out and grab me, either to mug my ass or to shoot me for not killing a long list of people. But rationally I knew that I had changed things. There wasn't some creepy-ass man playing the boogeyman and waiting to pounce. I proved that to myself when I saw Jen's name disappear from the list. I should be walking home without a care in the world.

I hurried up the stairs in the apartment building to get to our home. But suddenly something didn't feel right. If I had rewritten time, then why did I still have the hit list on that piece of paper? That hadn't disappeared. It only existed because someone had overheard who I was in Starbucks and came after me. We didn't go there this morning. No one overheard us.

I was wrong.

My hand was shaking as I slowly reached for the door knob. Something in my gut said that it might not be locked. I prayed that I was wrong as the cool metal handle touched my skin.

The locking mechanism gave no resistance. The handle kept twisting until my hand could rotate no more, and then I just let go. The door slowly swung inward. Instead of the stereotypical thriller scene with a dark room, the apartment had a couple table lamps lighting it up. I could see Meghan's backpack by the door sitting next to her shoes. She had come home. So at least I kept her safe that long. Maybe she just forgot to lock the door.

"Meghan?" I called, reluctantly.

The most probable thing was that she came home and forgot to lock the door or thought I was already home. I shut the door behind me as I walked more into the apartment. Her bedroom door was slightly ajar and there was a faint light coming from within. Okay, so she was here. Everything must have turned out just fine and she didn't answer me because she had headphones on and was listening to music. Totally.

I passed the empty pizza boxes on the kitchen counter as I head back towards the bedrooms. I tossed my backpack on the couch as I walked through.

"Meghan, I'm back. I got a story to tell you this time. You're not going to believe the day I had."

It was going to be a relief to get this out of my head and have her laugh at the crazy predicament we had fallen into. I pushed open her door, knowing that if it was already ajar that she wouldn't care, and I stopped cold when I saw what waited.

Meghan was laying on her bed, but it wasn't just that. Her hands were tied behind her back and she was nude. It wasn't that I never saw her strutting around in the buff before. It was that I never saw all those bruises and cuts all over her body before but that was the point now, wasn't it?

He wanted me to see how broken and tortured she had been. *He* wanted me to see and feel her pain. *He* wanted me to see how he had out-smarted me and killed my best friend in our own home. *He* wanted me to –

"Welcome home, Haley Brown," he whispered in my ear.

I hadn't heard or sensed him coming up behind me. I jumped away and turned to face him. In his left hand, I could see that he was carrying around the bloody steak knife that he had used to saw open my best friend's throat. The conundrum was how I didn't see the blood trail with all the drops of coming off it.

What was more of a shock was that he was still here, that he was in my apartment. I should have written him out of existence in my tiny world. Yet, here he was and there Meghan was, dead. How was this a super power if I couldn't save anyone?

"Confused, aren't you?" He chuckled. It had to be clear on my face. He was not supposed to be here nor know my name. "Thought you might be. You were such a bad girl, Haley Brown."

I took a step backwards as he took one closer. It didn't take a rocket science genius to know what was going to happen. There was a reason that he still held onto that steak knife. With the serrations, it was probably going to hurt a thousand times more. Not that I actually wanted to be stabbed and chopped up. Just an observation. And this guy was too smart to try and make my last request a paring knife or some other smooth blade design just so that I could have a two minute window to escape while his back was turned. No, that bullshittery wasn't going to work with him... not that I expected it to work with anyone.

"How did you find me?"

Might as well ask. I think at this point there was no harm in that. Well, this guy might think otherwise. He knew what I was able to do and must know that I could rewrite the past. Well, maybe he didn't. No, he had to if he knew I'd be surprised that he was still here and that my best friend was still murdered.

I couldn't think about that right now. Because I rewrote so much, the news of her death was hitting me just as hard as it had the first time. I couldn't let that linger in my brain when I needed all my neurons firing off to think of a way out of this.

"Same way I found you last time, Haley Brown."

What was his obsession with saying my whole name? Was it just the added creepy factor and to prove he knew who I was?

He tipped his head back and the hood of his sweatshirt fell off. I saw his face and it looked familiar, but at the same time it didn't. I couldn't place a name with a face. I couldn't remember where I might have ran into him when he wasn't going all psycho killer. I mean, if he always was a psycho killer, I'd probably remember him a little more. I doubt he really was going to tell me how or if I knew him. He probably just had similar facial features as someone else I knew or saw recently and it was messing with my brain. That or facing my death was causing a mental lapse. Yea, probably that one.

"And no, Haley Brown, I won't be telling you how that was exactly or even who I am." Although, with his head slightly cocked to the right, it seemed like he thought I should already know that last part.

As he kept getting closer, I was running out of places to go. I was being backed up into a corner, literally. He was between me and the door, and making me back up around Meghan's bed. I had to keep turning my head slightly so I couldn't see the bloody, gory mess that remained of my best friend; but that didn't stop me from stepping backwards into a pool of her blood.

My balance started slipping and I feared was going to fall. In my mind, landing in a pool of Meghan's blood was the worst possible scenario. Yea, priorities and all for the girl that pissed her pants. It was at that moment that he started rushing towards me, knife brazen and ready to hack into my skin.

My arms were flailing as I started falling backwards in my attempt to get away. My hands hit her nightstand and I latched on with a death grip, managing to keep myself from falling completely in the huge pool of red. But my legs split apart and my knees crashed onto the floor. I felt my pants soaking up Meghan's life and making them stick to my legs underneath the fabric.

With a murderous man rushing towards me, my dead best friend beside me, a corner behind my back, and a pool of blood beneath me, there was really only one way to go. I swung my foot underneath me and pushed myself out of a crouch on the floor, slipping the whole time. It was just enough to get me up high enough that my foot could step on the edge of the bed. I tried my best to get up and across the mattress without stepping on Meghan's dead – and kind of cold – body. If my feet weren't drenched enough before, the blood on top of her comforter made it worse, and my right leg slid out from underneath me. It was all in slow motion as my body fell. I landed sprawled across Meghan's torso. If, at that moment, I hadn't felt something dig around my ankle, I would have been mortified about what I was doing on top of my best friend's body.

"Haley Brown," he growled out.

The creep dug his fingernails into my ankle before dragging me back over Meghan's body towards him. My hands scrambled to get a grip on the blood-soaked comforter. I felt her long legs moving up under my body from my stomach to my chest to my arm pits. I knew it wouldn't be much longer before he had me off the bed and stabbed.

He choked up his hold on my leg, getting my knee almost under his elbow. I was way too close and he knew it by that growing smirk on his face. I watched as he raised the bloody steak knife. All he had to do was give one more good yank and I'd be ripe for the stabbing, and he was already starting to raise his stabbing arm.

I could feel my heart beating in my ears. I could feel my time left on earth ticking away. It was really starting to look like there was no way out of this. I could tell that reasoning with him was out of the question because I was apparently too dangerous to him now that I tried to write him out of my life.

"You should have just done what we said!"

I should have... I kicked his knife hand. He hadn't expected that and the knife went flying back towards the corner. I found a way out of this. He didn't have a weapon now. He couldn't hurt me. So why was he still pulling me closer? Had his intentions changed to some sexy time instead? My eyes glanced down towards his groin until I realized how ridiculous that was. By then I realized he was still armed. Literally.

His groin collided with mine as he yanked me hard. My hands held onto his... as he clamped down on my throat. My legs flailed on either side of him, not doing anything helpful. The edges of my vision were already starting to go dark as the air was disappearing from my lungs.

I was going to die here.

I was going to die here, alone, and with Meghan's dead body. I was going to die here knowing that I couldn't save or help anyone, let alone help myself. I was going to die here unless I figured a way out of this, and fast.

My hands fell away from his death grip around my throat. It only allowed him to squeeze my neck more now that I wasn't fighting. My arms felt weak from the lack of oxygen. My legs hung over the edge of the bed like two long, dead weights. He thought that he was going to win.

"Goodbye, Haley Brown."

I hated how he said my name. My fist balled up at my side. With one last hoorah, I shoved my hand down.

I struck gold.

"Bitch!"

I managed to connect with his fun dangly bits and had just enough strength left in my body to make it hurt. I coughed as air flooded my lungs again. His hands left my throat feeling raw and sore though, and I almost didn't want to breathe. I forced myself to take those first few deep breathes as I stared down between my legs at the hunched over man.

I needed to move before he recovered.

Rolling onto my side and then my front, I realized it was a terrible idea. I came face to face with Meghan's dead body again and the rush of emotions and guilt ravaged me for a moment too long. I forced myself up onto my elbows to get a grip and pull my body away from my attacker. But every handhold was difficult from the amount of blood making the bed slick. I could feel my wet clothes sticking to me on every part of my body, probably making me look like Carrie from that horrific prom scene. I got one leg underneath me and pushed myself to the other side of the bed, falling off and laying in a heap on the floor. But at least I had a whole bed between me and the creep. He couldn't stab me with a knife from over there.

"Haley..."

I scrambled to get up on my feet, but what I saw almost knocked me back down on my ass. He had reached behind him to pull out a gun that had been tucked in the back of his pants. A gun that was now pointed directly at me.

I swallowed hard. It was basically game over. I could outrun a crazy guy with a knife, but I wasn't fast enough to outrun a bullet. If I knew he was a terrible shot that couldn't hit the broadside of a barn while standing inside it, then I'd chance it and casually walk out of the bedroom. I had to assume that he knew how to use that. Either way I'd eventually be dead though.

It was a chance I was forced to take. I turned and bolted out the door, hearing wood splintering next to my ear as a bullet tore through the door frame.

He could shoot.

I spilled out into the hallway and tried to figure out where to run. I had three and a half seconds to make up my mind and get there before he made it around the bed and shot me dead. My bedroom was back down the short hallway and around the corner, connecting to the kitchen with our bathroom between us. I could dart into the porcelain tiled room and maybe make it through to my bedroom. There would be paper and pens in there and time to place an emergency call to the New York Police Department for back-up in case anything went array. The problem with my plan was if the creeper had taken any time to learn the layout of the apartment, he might know where I was heading and try to cut me off at the pass. I still had to take the chance.

I made it into the shared bathroom and slammed the door shut. And not a moment too soon. Three bullets tore holes in the door. I turned the lock in the doorknob handle, knowing it wasn't going to last too long. A well placed bullet or a couple shoulder thrusts into the door and it was done. I made it to the other side of the small bathroom when I heard footsteps falling hard.

The creeper had taken a tour of the apartment. He was coming for me.

I went to grab the notepad and pen off my nightstand, but didn't even get two steps outside the bathroom before he showed up in the doorway. I wasn't going to be able to grab my notepad and I was forever going to have to bob and dash between the bathroom and the bedrooms in order to escape him before he forced me into a dead end, calling checkmate.

The door that would have led to my bedroom slammed shut and the lock in the door knob handle engaged. I couldn't escape but I couldn't let him into the bathroom. I was trapped. There was no way out. Not even a window I could squeeze through, and I doubted anything could make it through the exhaust fan. That meant I had to somehow figure out a way to write from within this bathroom.

There was definitely no pen or pencil laying around. I doubted I could do anything with the one magazine that was scribbled on and noted for fashion pieces Meghan had her eye on and wanted. Too bad shopping for her birthday just got a whole lot easier – daisies or petunias. There was only toilet paper then to write on. Sure, I was scared shitless but there was nothing to scribble actual words down on that. None of it would be legible if I actually used my shit, let alone if I actually had the time to force my body to empty my bowels. Even then it was just ew…

I jumped, hearing his body ram against the door and then came the muffled curses from the other side. Time was running out. I needed something to write with and I needed to come up with a way out of this. My eyes scanned the sink countertop. Maybe Meghan left a stray pen or had one fall out of her purse accidentally. There was no such luck in that department. What I did see was a tube of toothpaste. There was a chance that I could use that. The question was how?

Toothpaste had the same problem as shit when it came to the toilet paper. I wouldn't be able to squeeze out a thin enough line of the cavity fighting gel to write out a way out for me. Wait... I glanced up and stared at my frazzled, bloody reflection in the mirror. I had a large canvas to write. I just needed the right words.

A bullet struck the toilet bowl behind me, and it crumbled a foot away from me. Guess the creep wasn't just going to wait around. He was going with Plan S – Plan Shoot. At any moment, one of his bullets could actually hit me. If I was lucky, it would only wound me and not kill me.

I grabbed the tube of toothpaste and screwed off the top. With one hand, I squeezed over half of what was left into my left hand to act as my palette, the same way an artist would when they were painting a masterpiece. My right index finger dipped into the cool mint gel and started to smear words on the mirror. As another bullet broke through the door and struck the edge of the shower, I hoped that this would work.

If I knew anything about guns, I would have been able to determine the model quickly when he first drew the weapon. I'd also would have been counting bullets and comparing it to the number of bullets held in one cartridge. I'd also know if the creeper had empty the magazine clip or not yet, and whether there was a short window to escape and sneak by while he changed that out... that was if he had another one hidden somewhere. But I didn't know weapons or guns pass what they were, like a classification. I knew a gun was a gun and knife was a knife. There was a break of silence before another bullet came through that door.

"Open up, Haley Brown!"

That was the one thing I wasn't going to do.

There wasn't enough time to think of the right words to rewrite the past or stop this future from happening. It meant that I needed to think of something to write to help me get out of this situation now and to write my future later. I could write that cops were on the way and save myself the time and hassle of doing that with just a few words. But they would probably take creeper guy into police custody and question him – which he'd be stupid to answer anything – until a lawyer got him out. Then he'd be back after me, one way or another. I had to be the way that this ended.

I pulled open the cabinet under the sink and reached up to find a gun taped there. Ripping it through the tape, I checked the magazine clip to find it full. Hopefully I wouldn't need more than six bullets for my new glock handgun.

Taking a deep breath, I stepped inside the shower-tub combo and hunkered down. I was praying that the actual body of the tub would keep me safe from any bullets he'd be firing off. All I needed to do was camp out and wait for him to make that first move. If he didn't come through that door, then there'd be a police officer knocking it down to save me. Either way, someone was coming through that door and – for the first time – I hoped I saw this creep.

I heard the door cracking as someone tried to break through with their shoulder and then the quick, louder thud of a foot connecting to the door. My hands were shaking as I waited.

"Haley Brown!" He snarled. Yea, he was really pissed. "I'm going to make you pay for that. Such a bitch…"

My ears started ringing as shots kept coming and then the silence hit. I glanced up at to watch in shock and horror as a hand reached through the chunk of door missing by the handle. Between the bullets and his own stubborn strength, the creep managed to break through. His hand found the door knob and the locking mechanism there. He turned it, unlocking the door and then rotated the handle. The door swung open slowly, but I was sure that was his intent. He wanted to scare me and make me fear him. He wanted me to beg for my life and run from the death he was here to deliver to me.

I knew that he wouldn't be able to see me right away, but he could see the door on the other side of the bathroom. He could see that it was still closed and locked. He would know that I was hiding somewhere. It was probably just assumed that I was hiding somewhere less "in sight" as the bathtub, but that was cliché for you.

His footsteps sounded both cautious and commanding. They came slowly and I knew he was looking for any sign of me. He was also trying to judge and pick out all the hiding places I could be holed up in. I glanced down at the gun in my lap to make sure the safety was off. That would be the worst possible thing to happen.

He took a step closer, but stopped right at the edge of the bathtub. Looking up, I could see the stubble on his jawline and the gun he held out in front of him through the gap between the wall and the shower curtain. Any second, he'd turn or glance down and spot me. This was the best chance I had to shot him. It was just that he was so close and I didn't want his blood on me too. That would just be wrong and disgusting.

I slowly lifted my gun, so that the sudden movement wouldn't catch his eye. I had the shot lined up to hit him just about his left eye socket that would end this madness. My finger rested on the trigger while I took one last deep breath to calm me slightly. My heart stopped beating for a second when his gaze inevitably turned down towards me. I saw his eyes go wide and read it on his face that he was going to try to make an escape. It would be an escape that wouldn't last long now that he knew I was trapped and knew of the only hiding place in the bathroom. He'd get away, regroup, and come after me again.

I squeezed the trigger.

The gun went off, sending a small kickback through my arms. But it was the loud sound and the way it bounced around off the tiles that messed me up. I was in a bit of a daze as I looked for my would-be killer and found him leaning against the sink counter, holding his face.

"Fucking cunt. You're going to pay for that! We won't let you live now!"

Blood was dripping down through his fingers and I knew I had hit him. With him standing though, I knew it wasn't enough to kill him. He must have moved just enough to prevent that. But that meant he'd be ready and able to come back at me. Now there was a direct path between us within this bathroom. That both was a curse and a blessing. It meant he had a clean shot on me, but I had a clean shot on him as well.

I raised my gun and aimed at the larger target of his chest. I knew this was wrong in my head – to kill someone – but I knew this was definitely self-defense. The gun exploded in my hand, sending a bullet clear across the room in a split second. The dark stain in his black shirt was growing fast.

Finally, he dropped the gun. He fell to his knees. For a moment, I felt bad and pity for him that it had to come to this. And then that feeling was gone. This was the man that killed my best friend and had wanted to kill my sister and me as well. I watched as his weakening body fell forward.

I stepped out of the tub and carefully around his body until the back of my legs touched the sink countertop. I kicked his gun away from him and towards the broken toilet. The amount of blood already on the floor was a good indication that he wouldn't have the strength to be able to grab the weapon, let alone take aim and shoot me from down there.

I looked down upon him like he had looked down upon me earlier. He deserved to know that I had out bested him. He deserved to know that I wasn't going to cower and cry over what he forced me to lose. He deserved to know that I had done this and that I had done this with words he wanted to use me for.

His eyelids seemed to be getting heavier and he had a harder time keeping them open. His chest wasn't moving so much. It seemed like he was fading fast. One thing was for sure though, from where he laid at my feet. I'm sure he could see the words written behind me on the mirror as he struggled to take his last breaths.

The cops are coming. I find a gun. I know how to shoot. I live.

I could hear sirens now. It would only be a couple moments before the police came up and through the front door. They could catch me with the gun that killed this man, but I couldn't let them see those words written on the mirror. I grabbed the hand towel beside the sink and swiped chunks of the gel substance off. There definitely were smears and there was no way someone wasn't going to notice that, but the actual real words were gone. I could lie and say I accidentally squeezed the hell out of it and the tube of toothpaste exploded on the mirror.

My hands weren't shaking as much as I thought they would be as I set the gun down on the counter next to the sink. I leaned back against the sink and stared down at the man, dead, on my bathroom floor. Somehow he had known who I was. For some reason, he had wanted me so bad and wanted me for such horrible things. I should have felt at ease, but I didn't. He had kept saying "we" over and over, almost as much as he said my full name.

He wasn't alone in all this.

Chapter Six

It felt like my life was just ending even though it was supposed to be just beginning. I had no family and I had no friends. I had no past and really no real future. I just had my life. I could stick it out and walk around on campus, hearing what they were saying about Meghan and me, and complete my degree. But that seemed more pointless now. I had only selected my major to keep from having homework that was heavily written or a language degree where one slip-up from me would change how the world spoke and create monumental errors and misconnects. I couldn't even use what I'd worked so hard for these last four years for any real job.

Where did that leave me now?

I wish I knew. I just knew that I wasn't behind bars, and I wasn't dead. I even knew who had attacked me and killed Meghan.

His name was Dominic Erikson and he was from York, which was a couple towns over from mine. Being relatively the same age as me meant that maybe we could have run into each other at sporting events, but I hadn't really gone to any of that. I was an outcast while it seemed like he was the star of the track and field teams. But that wasn't the only thing we had in common. Apparently he had been an economics major here at Columbia. Our paths most likely wouldn't have crossed but it was strange to have someone always being so close to running parallel to myself and not having run into them at least once. I had even asked if there was a connection that the police had made between him and Meghan but there was nothing there either. While I knew his name and how he came to be on this campus, I didn't know his story or why he came after me or who "we" was. I didn't know why he was even obsessed with my name, and that was what dug into me the worst.

I started to hate my name. It brought nothing but trouble for me lately. The more and more time that past made me more and more *The Writer*. Adam had been right. I had just needed to leave, but our plan to run away to the big city wasn't far enough. I had to run from it all... somehow.

Walking out of the police department, I headed down the street and turned the corner to head downtown. There really wasn't any point going home. Besides, the police were there to investigate what happened and the coroner was there to take Meghan's body out of the apartment. I did feel bad for her family though, but I knew there was really no way I could have saved her. I had tried.

Would her family blame me?

I was the one that survived. I was there, and maybe if I came home sooner I could have stopped it from happening. At the end of the day, though, Meghan was still dead because of me. Dominic wouldn't have known about her or gone after her if it wasn't for me. I had unknowingly brought something down upon us.

I killed Meghan.

I couldn't go back home.

Sticking my hands in my pant pockets, I felt the police secretary's pen that I swiped and the business card of the detective that had interrogated me and was looking into Meghan's murderer. Well, not that there was much more to look into because they had their murder already. There was no reason to look further other than my word that the creeper had insinuated that there was another person in this.

There was no particular destination in mind as I wandered the streets. I remembered my time on the streets as I passed by food vendors on the street corners that never gave me the time of day or their burnt unsellable goods. I remembered starving and begging. I remembered the masses that just ignored me.

I pulled out my stolen goods and scribbled on the back of the business card for a notepad. The notepad showed up a few feet ahead of me on the sidewalk. I stopped and bent to pick it up. Now I had the means to make things really change. Crumbling up the business card that I'd never need to use again, I tossed it in a trash can along the way as I headed nowhere.

Taxi cabs swerved and cars honked as the world kept moving. I still had no idea where I was going or what I was going to do. I could erase myself from history again and write a new identity. I could try to figure out who was after me too. I guess that would be a good thing to figure out. If I didn't eliminate the threat to my life and everything I touched and everyone I met, then there was no point in moving on with my life. I needed to figure out a way to make that happen.

There was no way that I could go back and follow Dominic through the past five years to find out whom he talked to and whom he got involved with. I didn't even know if I could write and request a book about his life or force him to have written a diary that I could collect somewhere, or even for the name of his partner or group to pop into my head. That all seemed too easy and probably not probable.

There wasn't much I knew about Dominic, which mostly led me right to a dead end. I was going to need to make some assumptions. Like I could assume that Dominic had a criminal background, seeing as he killed so easily. Whoever he had been working with probably had a criminal background as well. It was going to be hard for me to get a complete list or gather that knowledge myself. I wasn't about to turn into a criminal to end this; however, I wasn't above writing them into police custody and stacking evidence against them to convict them with life terms.

So that left me with limited options. There had to be a way to find postings about the latest criminals. It probably sounded old school, but there was always the post offices. They seemed to always have posters with the wanted criminals, but that was locally and seemed to probably be something that only existed in movies. The easiest way would probably be to pull out my phone and do an internet search for the most wanted criminals or criminal activity near my location or my hometown. But if they somehow managed to find me, who's to say it wasn't through tracking my internet searches or some kind of online hacking with computer viruses and technology stuff that I wouldn't even begin to understand because I had no idea, really, how any of it worked. The conspiracy theorist had to be right about something... right? So technology was off limits and the post office was most likely a dead end.

The wind kicked up a bit and smacked a stray sheet from an abandoned newspaper against my leg. I stared down at the piece of paper that tried to wrap itself around me. That gave me an idea. Sure it wasn't foolproof or comprehensive, and it probably would get me nowhere but I had a start. I could scour through newspapers. There'd definitely be news articles about murders, arson, theft, and the crazy stuff like streaking nude through a busy subway station.

I could start there and work my way up. There was no doubt that the person or persons working with Dominic weren't going to show up in today's news. I could eventually start working my way back through old newspapers, but I wanted to focus on the recent times and what this person was up to now. They probably had lackeys to do their dirty work. But what happened when they didn't have lackeys anymore? Eventually they were going to have to get their hands dirty again or start recruiting hardcore. If they took matters into their own hands, then I'd get them when their name popped up in the headlines. If they took the passive route to rebuild their numbers, then the New York Police Department would probably notice and stick someone undercover or something and take down this mystery person that way. I could just write them into finding evidence against this person if the news showed they were struggling to prosecute.

So I just needed to find newspapers.

There were a couple stray sections of newspaper crumbled up, discarded, soaked, torn, blowing in the wind. Newspaper littered the streets. It was just an unreliable way to find the information that I needed when I couldn't guarantee I'd get a criminal news section or anything about court dates and servings. I would have to buy all the newspapers I needed for that and it would cost a small fortune that I just didn't have. I'd have to think of something else.

But while I waited for the crossing light in my path to change, a man walked up beside me with a shopping cart. Glancing over at it, slightly confused for a moment what three foot mess was next to me, I saw sorted piles of newspapers, aluminum cans, plastic bags, spoons. I found a junker.

It was something I heard a couple homeless people toss around one night when I was warming up by one of the street barrel fires. They were talking about how they wanted to break into the caste of being a junker. Scrounging around for recyclables and making some profit off others' discards seemed like a sweet deal if you did that at night and begged during the day. But it was harder than anyone knew. There were only certain rich – well, non-homeless people – that would take the goods and there had to be some kind of relationship and agreement established with them. Then there were the other veteran junkers that would tamper with your stash if you crossed into their territories or were too green to know not to turn your back on your cart. It was a rougher life than just begging, and the few that dabble only collected cans that they could return in grocery stores' automated can machines.

I wondered how much he was getting to junk newspapers. They didn't logically seem to be more profitable than recycling soda cans. I could probably get away with asking if the couple bucks in my pocket would buy me his current stack, seeing as I probably wouldn't see this homeless man again. I had my notepad and, technically, I could write him just giving them away to me. Or I could write him into the fortunes of having a paying job, a home, and access to clean, fresh food. That would be worth its weight in gold if this homeless man actually would believe that and do everything I asked based just on my word. It would also mean telling someone else about me and possibly letting the wrong people know who I am again. There was no one left that I cared about that would be attached to me, but there could still be deaths to weight heavy on my conscience.

"You got a contract?" I asked, keeping my gaze forward now.

The crosswalk light turned green but neither of us made a move to cross the street.

A gravelly voice told me, "No."

It was said reluctantly though. I doubted many people knew the lingo of being homeless, much less talk to the homeless in general. To the masses, they weren't seen as still being human. This man probably expected a girl like me to see him as a threat, a nuisance, and to scurry away before he could even give a little push on his cart.

Instead, I turned and faced him. For the first time, I actually saw who I was striking up a conversation with in hopes of making a deal. He had to be about six feet tall when he wasn't hunched over, and I'm sure he once had a handsome face before the salt-and-pepper beard and scruff took over his haggard face. The top of his head was covered in a makeshift hat from the left leg of some holey pair of pants. In another life or another dimension, he probably could have played the role of my dad with his age. His olive complexion didn't match my own skin tone, but that wasn't really the problem here. He looked like he had a tough life but he was managing it.

"I'm in the business of looking for newspapers. I couldn't help but to notice you have a good stock of it. I'm not sure if it's been promised to someone else, but I'd like to buy it from you." I watched as he shifted a little uncomfortably between his feet for a moment. "I don't want to break contracts you have with someone else, but I'd like to hire you. I can pay you weekly for spare newspapers you pick up. It would be pretty long-term and at the end of it, if things work out, I can promise you a bonus like no other."

His face was hard to read. He stared down at his cart, mostly, and I knew that I made him uncomfortable just by acknowledging that he existed. Maybe that alone would cost me this junker.

"A man in Brooklyn has a claim on them... and the subway has been getting expensive." His quiet voice held out a bit of hope that I had him as my source in this crazy endeavor. "But these are his, miss. I can't break my contract. And not to insult you – you are a pretty lady – but I don't think you would really want to give me *that* at the end of this. I would disappoint."

Oh. I, um, actually hadn't thought he'd take what I said about the good job bonus *that* way. I tried not to freak out or come off as shooting him down for just being homeless. That kind of a bonus wasn't on the table for anyone.

"I was talking about getting a way for you to be off the streets and safe. I know I may not look like it, but I can find a way to give you that and change things for you." Now I accidently give him too much hope. "But unfortunately, that starts with getting your newspapers. I can understand if you can't break your contract. I know you won't let me talk to him, and it wouldn't be right when it's your business. But if he decided to end your contract, would you give me your stock every week? We can work out what I'd pay you for them."

I had no doubt that this Brooklyn man who held the newspaper contract would back out. Especially when I would write it happening. I would just need a few more details to ensure it.

When the homeless man nodded, I outstretch my hand. It clearly wasn't something he was used to doing. Hopefully that helped sway him to my side – the fact I treated him as a human. I knew what it had been like, but I'd never tell this man that.

"My name's Meghan." Claiming my best friend's name would be a good reminder as to why I'm doing this.

He reached out and shook my hand. "Marshall."

"Nice to meet you, Marshall." I smiled a little as I shook his hand. "Can I meet you here Tuesday whether the man breaks or keeps your newspaper contract? I'll be in this part of town around lunchtime and I'd like to buy you a meal for at least listening to me."

"But I might not be able to tell you yes..." The shimmer of hope for a hot meal was quickly dying in his mind with that revelation.

"It doesn't matter. If you can't, then you can't. Maybe you'd know another junker that could help me. Either way, I don't really have cash on me right now to give you for your time."

He seemed to be considering it. I'd really hate to force Marshall into seeing me again. Slowly, he nodded.

I glanced up at the street corner. "105th and Lexington." It would be a little bit of a walk each week when I made it happen, but it was probably for the best to have it on this side of Central Park and away from campus. "I'll see you Tuesday."

Marshall didn't say anything as I walked away. I hoped he'd be there in a few days.

I headed back towards Central Park, thinking it would be a good place to find somewhere relatively quiet and alone. I needed time to think and to write. The day was leaving me, but I couldn't go home. I didn't have a home anymore and I wasn't about to go begging in the dorms for a classmate to let me take up the couch. Not that I really knew any of my classmates or where they lived. I could crash at a frat house during one of their parties, but then there was the possibility of a drunken man-boy encounter.

I shivered involuntarily.

I'd at least cut through the park then. It was the quickest way back to campus. Along the way, I'd stop and write Marshall out of his contract with the Brooklyn guy. I'd scribble down some sentences about me and then just enjoy the autopilot ride of fate for the night. Yea, that actually sounded really nice. I could really use a carefree night where I had no control, other than the control I had right now when I wrote my future.

After crossing one of the hundreds of foot bridges, I veered off on the north-west path. The streetlights through the park were just warming up and faintly staring to glow in the evening air. Pausing beneath one, I pulled out my notepad and the NYPD pen.

Marshall, the homeless man, delivers his inventory of newspapers to his Brooklyn buyer. The Brooklyn buyer takes his last stack and lets Marshall out of their contract. Marshall decides that he'll meet with the person he knows as Meghan on Tuesday and take the job. On the subway train, he finds five dollars.

Haley Brown walks quickly through Central Park and towards a frat party. She walks in and manages to find an unoccupied, clean bedroom. She locks the door and goes to sleep. No one bothers her. In the morning, she is able to leave without anyone seeing her or knowing that she was there. There's leftover pizza on the kitchen table and a couple cans of soda for her to take.

If I was going to take care of Marshall, I had better take care of myself too. Tucking away my notepad, my feet started carrying me along the path. I knew that I'd find a frat house and get a good night's sleep without being raped or disturbed by the owner of the bed I'd be stealing. Those words also granted me a little piece of mind for tomorrow when I'd be back on the streets and on my own.

That was something I was going to have to deal with and work around. I couldn't live on the streets again. I couldn't exactly write myself into riches in this town without some hoity-toity uppity person questioning my pedigree. But I could help myself get back up again. That would be what I did tomorrow. Then in a couple days, I'd have Marshall helping me get criminals off the street as I try to lock away the person that stole my life away from me. But my zealous mood was faltering. In a city of so many, there were so few in the park at this time. It was quiet and relaxing. I almost wanted to spend the night here. The reality was though that I had a greater chance of becoming the victim to someone else's nefarious plans. By day, Central Park was great but by night it was a danger zone. So I kept walking until I arrived on the front stoop of my shelter tonight.

The party was really raging when I walked into Omega Psi. There were a couple kegs smack dab in the center of the living room. Rainbow strobe lights flashing. Girls and guys practically naked all over the... no, there were definitely two naked girls over there. I didn't even want to know how much they had to drink, if they actually needed to have drank anything to strip and strut their goodies.

I moved towards the stairs and took them a two at a time. My body was just starting to feel incredibly heavy from all the emotions and death and danger and thinking and walking I had done today. I just wanted to pass out for a long while. Heading towards what must have been my clean, vacant room, I spotted a small t-shirt tossed on a lampshade. Picking it up, I took the risk of holding it to my nose, only to find out that it was clean. Yea, it was a pukey shade of olive green but it was clean and not blood-soaked red. I wish the police department had given me something else to wear or at least washed my clothes. I would have worn orange – black strips or not – unless that was all just in the movies too.

It didn't matter if I slammed the bedroom door shut or not. With the music downstairs, no one would have heard or noticed it. This wasn't my room or my house, so I closed it quietly and turned the lock in the door handle. Stripping out of my bloody shirt, I pulled the "borrowed" one on over my head. It didn't seem like the guy I was borrowing his room from had jeans in my size or had a girl in his room lately. Meaning I was out of luck. I pulled off the dried pants and added them to the growing heap on the floor of blood spatter clothes. It was a miracle that Marshall even talked to me, after realizing what I must have looked like to him.

I crawled in under the sheets and sighed. This felt like heaven after the day I had. The pillow was soft underneath my head and everything just seemed to be perfect. It couldn't have been long before I was passed out and my mind, gratefully, shut off.

The next morning, I managed to find my way to the bathroom and snuck a quick shower. Yes, it was extremely risky. But I was covered with dried blood and feeling grimy. Besides, I wrote that no one would see or know I was here. As long as it stayed morning and hadn't flipped to afternoon, I should be fine. Plus, hot water felt divine!

There was still the issue of clothing once I got out. I grabbed a towel to wrap around my body and headed back to the room I had commandeered. There was nothing usable here nor anything I had seen anything on my short walk from the shower. I plopped down on the bed and pulled out my notepad. I needed clothes immediately. I also needed some cash and a place to start my new life, but I could write those things when I was out of this place and not running the risk of being caught.

In the dresser drawer in the room I'm occupying, there's a black backpack with my sized clothes and the essential travel items. In the front pocket are a couple snacks and a small composition set. In the one of the pants, there's a pocket with an envelope of cash. When I leave, no one will be around inside the house. There's a pizza box with a few uneaten slices of pepperoni and a couple cans of root beer left on a side table next to the couch in the living room.

I had to step around a couple piles of stacked clothing and push away a box of whey protein shake mix, but I finally got to the drawer and opened it.

"For the love of god!"

I slammed the thing shut and tried to calm down before my heart pounded right out of my chest. That was something I should have seen coming. Ugh, my eyes felt violated. I didn't want to open that drawer again, but it had all my stuff in it. Slowly, I pulled back the drawer, trying to keep my eyes off the collection of porn magazines that litter the top of what I hoped was more porn magazines and maybe a spare sweatshirt or something. My hand touched the distinctly different texture of canvas and pulled it out of the smooth, used-feeling piles of paper. Shutting the drawer, I breathed a sigh of relief that that was done.

To set my mind at ease, I checked the outside of my black backpack just to make sure nothing rubbed off. It was a small relief. Pulling the zipper open in the single large compartment, I took inventory as I dug around the contents. It was going to be nice to be in clean panties and my own clothes again. I found the bra first and was glad that they matched the bottoms. Now came the stressful part.

Standing up, I stripped out of my borrowed shirt and underwear. At any moment, a horny frat guy might walk in and get the shock of having a living, breathing woman in his room instead of copious amounts of porn in a stash. I'd have to live with the guilt over that boner.

I quickly pulled on my underwear and borrowed shirt before taking a breath to go back and see what was in the backpack of goodies. There were a couple pairs of jeans that had been written into existence, a hooded sweatshirt, a couple tops, granola and snack bars, bottle of water, deodorant, a notebook and pens, a roll of toilet paper, and a bank cash envelope. Seemed to cover all the basics but dental hygiene... no, wait, there was a toothbrush and a travel size tube of toothpaste.

Turning my used, bloody clothes inside out, I stashed them in the bottom of the backpack. When I got the chance, I'd wash them and have another stash of clean clothes for another day. I wasn't sure how fast I'd be able to put my life back together so, just in case, I needed everything I had. For now, I didn't want crusty blood breaking off and getting everywhere.

I slung the backpack over my shoulder and headed out of the borrowed bedroom. True to what I wrote, there was no one around and the pizza and soda were right where it should have been. I tucked the cans away in my bag and looked around for paper plates or napkins to wrap up the leftover pizza. I didn't want cheese and sauce all over my clean clothes either. I managed to find a couple paper plates and a rubber band for a makeshift container. Now I had a meal for the day. Everything was coming up right for me.

I walked out the front door and ran smack dab into the thick chest of a man. When I stepped back, I realized that I missed his leathery musk scent. Crap! No one was supposed to see me.

"You running from Chase?"

Oddly, it didn't seem like he was phased by our run-in. But who was Chase? Was he the guy whose room I took? I could just say I was and play it off. If this guy talked to the one called Chase, my cover might be blown and then they might actually try to come looking for me. And I was done with people looking for me.

Shaking my head, I tried to step around him but there just wasn't the room on the front steps with his larger frame. "I just passed out last night at the party." Well, it was a half-truth. There had been a party and I had passed out. I just wasn't invited or attended said party. "I was just going to go now." If he let me…

"So you didn't shack up with Chase last night?"

Why was he so stuck on that? I shook my head, but it didn't seem like he was buying it. Why would this guy care what this Chase did? Not unless they were…

"Is Chase your boyfriend?" I asked.

For a moment, he looked pissed but then just erupted with laughter. "Naw, he's my brother and a douche. I just didn't know if he was giving me his sloppy seconds again or setting me up on a blind date." He took a step up closer to me. "I hope you're not my blind date 'cos it would suck if you were running out on me already."

I… I didn't know how to respond to that. Okay, clearly he wasn't gay. Obviously, he liked me. Damn, because he smelled good.

"Come on. Let's go back inside and actually get to know each other before you book it out of here. I mean, I'm not that ugly. Am I?"

I shook my head again, slowly. He definitely wasn't ugly. But that seemed to have been the wrong answer. It had his arm around my back, leading me back inside the house I was trying to escape. Because I had left and now I

114

was back again, the words I wrote last night were kind of void at this point. Someone was going to see me and now they might remember that I look familiar. Either way, this guy might just say that I was here last night and then even worrying over being recognized was pointless.

He led me upstairs without me really realizing where we were going. My feet just moved with him as he talked a little about his brother and these blind dates or maybe it was about his brother and what classes we were taking. Or was it about my tastes in porn? I stopped in the doorway when I realized what room he had taken me too. He left me standing where I was and went to drop his duffel bag at the foot of his bed and then pulled up his bedsheets.

"Shit. Chase must have let someone use my room again." He groaned and sniffed the sheets. If he got close to me, would he realize that I was the one to crash here? "Doesn't smell like they fucked in here."

He shrugged and sat down on the bed, waving me over. I didn't move. This was either going to lead to someone fucking in his room or something really bad. Maybe if I owned up to being here last night he'd be too embarrassed by what he just said and I could finally get out of here.

"Actually, I slept here last night. The party was going on and it was quieter here. I just saw the bed, crawled in, and passed out."

I waited for him to backpedal on what he just said or to get upset or to make a move to force me to sit beside him on the bed. Instead, he just kind of smiled.

"All the better then. I'd rather have a pretty girl like you keeping my sheets warm."

Oh, god... did he just say that? If I really was his blind date that he thought I was, I would have been out the door. Gone. Never looking back.

"Fuck! That came out creepier than I meant. I meant that I'd rather have you sleeping in here than a pair of fuck bunnies messing up my shit, getting wasted and puking up the alcohol they managed not to spill in here."

"Sounds like you know from personal experience."

"You have *no* idea," he half chuckled. "My name's Carter. Carter Hathorn."

Oh... this was really happening, wasn't it? He was introducing himself and I wanted to lie. But he went to Columbia and would know I was lying if I claimed to be Meghan, like I had for Marshall. Everyone would know her name by the end of the weekend, and they'd know she was dead. I either had to use my real name or pull a name out of my ass and play that role until I got out of this guy's life.

"Haley." Keep it short and simple. There had to be other Haleys on campus, so maybe he wouldn't make the connection to me. That and he wouldn't have my last name to pass onto some other crazy psycho killer.

He got up and walked over. Carter must have seen how hesitant I was to have him closer. It was probably a blow to his ego. Then again, maybe it was a common reaction if he had that much porn in his bottom dresser drawer. He stuck his hands in his pant pockets and I kind of got the idea it was the same thing as if he held up his hands in front of him – this was a safe zone.

"Well, Haley, nice to meet ya. I'm glad you ran into me." Oh, he just had to bring that up! And Carter clearly saw that it pestered me because he chuckled. "How about I take you out tonight for dinner?"

I stared at him. Did he really just ask me out? We knew nothing about each other except that he collected porn and I didn't watch where I was going. And what was I going to wear out on a date? I had what was in my backpack and nothing more unless I wanted to relive the horror back in the apartment. Well, that was if the police would let me in to grab some of my stuff. And even if I did have something to wear, I had a lot to get done today like giving myself someplace to live and figuring out what my future was going to be.

"Well? Do you want to?"

Crap.

It looked like he'd genuinely be hurt if I turned him down. Yea, we met awkwardly and he just brought me back to his room for nothing. I doubted he took me up here just to ask me out. I'd be lying if I said I didn't find him a little attractive. And it was only one date.

"Sure, yea. But I can't tonight. I have plans already." Well, I was going to make plans. A lot of plans. "How about you pick the place and time and just text me where to meet you?" I'd have to give him my phone number, but oh well.

He still seemed a little nervous as he rubbed the back of his neck. "How about I come pick you up and we'll go together?"

Ha! Yea, pick me up where? An active crime scene?

117

"It's kind of long story, but it will be a lot easier just to meet you somewhere." A long story that I hoped he wasn't about to ask me to tell.

Carter nodded slightly and I wondered if he thought – knew – I was blowing him off. "I guess I can do that. Just give me your phone for a sec."

"What?" *Crap*. Why would he want that? Was he going to...?

"I want to put my number in your phone so you can't claim to have lost my number. Then I'm going to call my phone so I got your number." He held out his hand and waited for me to cough up the phone. "You don't really trust people, do you?"

I scoffed at that while I dug my cell phone out of my back pocket and put it in his hand. "I trust people," I grumbled. I trusted them... just not right now and not some strange guy trying to pick me up. If only Carter knew what I had just been through these last couple of days.

He brought up my contacts and created a new one for himself. Just what Carter was putting in there was something I'd have to check out later. It seemed like it was more than just his name and number with how long he typed. When he smiled and took a selfie, yea, I knew it. He really didn't want me forgetting him.

"Scared I'm going to forget what you look like?"

He chuckled. "Naw. Actually, I shouldn't have done that. You'll see how ugly and weird I am when I call and block my number."

"You're not ugly." I rolled my eyes. "Jury's still out on the weird part though."

Carter just smiled as he hit the green button on the screen and called his phone. Queen's Bohemian Rhapsody started going off in his back pocket. Instead of pulling out his phone, he simply ended the call on mine.

"Well, seeing as I'm not ugly, I guess you can have this back now." He handed over my phone. "Just don't send me any goofy or weird photos of you to try and scare me off," he teased.

Carter was trying to bait me! The smug guy knew my phone could take photos. He probably just wanted photos of me... but I had to give him props for not asking for nudes. That definitely would have shot his chances to hell. Maybe he wasn't really like that, or maybe Carter already had enough nudes in his collection.

"You're scaring me off now." I rolled my eyes and turned to head towards the front door.

He was following behind me, laughing. "You know, you're pretty awesome for a hookup from Chase. I don't mean to keep calling you that. It's just that I'm really surprised that I actually kind of like you."

I paused on the steps and looked back over my shoulder at him. "But you don't even know me."

"You're cute and funny and willing to give me a chance. I can tell by your outfit that you're not some high-maintenance bitch. You're not a crazy sorority sister, otherwise we'd have met *long* ago." I let that comment go. From what I knew, Carter was either set-up with them and ditched or met through from Greek events on campus. "Your perfect night is probably staying in and binge watching something on Netflix. You like your bed unfucked and your pillows firm. Either you really passed

119

out 'cos you were tired last night or you don't flop and flail around in your sleep."

Putting my hands on my hip and turning to face him, I tried to give him that bored kind of stare. While he was hitting the nail on the head for all of those things, it was hard to believe that he actually knew that and wasn't just take wild stabs in the dark.

"And how do you know that?"

Carter smirked a little. It was annoying, but also cute. "Well, you just confirmed that all that was right." Shit. "And you didn't make the bed. The covers were pushed down, but only like you got out of bed. No pillows went flying across the room. And who wants someone fucked in their bed?"

Okay, he had me on that last one.

"Aren't frat boys supposed to be stupid drunks?" I shook my head and headed for the door. I would have felt a little bit bad for calling this decent enough guy stupid and drunk. Well, actually, I was stereotyping everyone else he knew and not directly him. But he let out a laugh as he walked me to the door.

"Not all of us are so stupid or bad. Who do you think they send out for the liquor? Someone has to know what's the good stuff to get."

Touché.

"So I guess I'll just call you or text you later?" Again, there was a little nervousness there. This guy wasn't exactly what I expected him to be.

"Yea. And if I don't answer right away, don't freak out or be that clingy guy. I'm not going to ditch you. I just have a lot to do tonight." Where'd that come from?

Carter nodded his head like he knew exactly what I was talking about or, hell, if I gave him my whole To-Do list to prove it. "Guess I don't have to be clingy if you're promising to actually go out with me."

It made me wonder a little what the other girls had done to Carter for him to say something like that. I also didn't expect to think about thinking about that. Why did it matter to me? It wasn't like I was really going to date him. This was just to get me out of today's mess with him having caught me as the perpetrator of his bed last night.

And it felt kind of awkward now as we stood at the door. It wasn't like it was a date and I was expected to kiss him goodbye. It also didn't seem like a comfortable thought to just leave like nothing happened or like I was his study buddy. I actually kind of knew him now and, yes, kind of liked him. I probably would have given him my phone number to break the awkwardness if he already didn't take it.

"So, I'll just be go-" His lips cut me off.

Carter's lips were so nice as he kissed me. His hands started off holding my face gently as he backed me up against the front door. His hair was oddly soft as my fingers ran through it. And he... What the hell was I doing?

I tore my mouth from his and couldn't understand this weird feeling I got. It was almost like pain and I almost was regretting doing it. It didn't make any sense. Carter shouldn't have kissed me, and I shouldn't have like it...

"Why did you do that?" ... *but I did like it.*

He was trying to read me. My voice had been too quiet for him really to hear the panic or regret or wanting in my tone. I hadn't actually pushed him away, even though my fingers were no longer enjoying the feeling of those dark locks of hair.

"Because I wanted to." Carter didn't hesitate to answer that one. He did even seem a little nervous about admitting that. "And I want to kiss you again, Haley."

Oh, crap...

I kind of wanted him to kiss me again too but there was no telling what that would lead to and I had something, I think, that I needed to be doing right now. Something pushed against my back and reminded me of where I was and why. A door knob. Yea, I needed to get a place to live and a new life.

And now, someone was pounding on the door. "Damn it! Someone come move the fucker passed out! I wanna get in!" The knocking got even louder behind my head.

"Shit..." Carter let me move out from in front of the door and grabbed the handle to open it just as some guy was starting to go back to his assault on the door.

"What the fuck, Hathorn?" The guy shoved his way in. "Fucking ass, locking me out and..."

The new guy stopped when he saw me. He had been heading upstairs to the bedrooms but now his attention was what was on the ground floor. I wished it wasn't. I could see the switch from douche to playa go off in his head before he even tried to lay on the charm with me.

"And who's this pretty young thang?"

Oh, god, gag me with a spoon.

"None of your damn business," Carter threw back.

There was something between these two? I could feel the tension coming off Carter. Had this other guy had done something to him in the past? Maybe stole a girlfriend? Didn't seem too farfetched with the sleazy pick-up line I was getting.

"Aw, come on, Hathorn. Introduce me to your pretty little lady friend."

"I don't want him to and I don't want to even talk to you. You are not my type, nor do I like anything about you, and right now you're wasting my time with Carter." I watched as two faces turned to stare at me, jaws on the floor. Well, hopefully being that honest wasn't going to bring a shitstorm down on Carter later.

I turned my attention back to the man in front of me and put on the best innocent smile I could. "Text me later, babe. I'll make sure to stay up for it." To add sugar to the honey, I leaned in and kissed him on the cheek. My lips felt a little stubble there and my mind wanted to drift to images of what he'd look like with a beard and... must stay focused. "I'll see you tomorrow for date night."

I winked before disappearing out the front door before either of the guys could regain proper brain function to process what just happened. Did I feel guilty over putting that douche in his place? No. Did I realize that I might have accidentally lead Carter on and was going to hurt his feelings later? Yes, a little, and definitely too late. It was something that would have to wait until later for me to beat myself up over. I had a lot to figure out and write and I needed to put all my attention to that problem first.

I headed back to Central Park. Not just because it was really the only place I could go in this city, but it was the only place I could and felt like going to. I knew there'd be a bench or table somewhere for me to sit down at and take time to just do me.

There was a lot of people in the park today. Guess the weekends had a habit of being that way. My thoughts kept bringing me back to the Bethesda Fountain as the place I wanted to be. I could sit and just listen to the water and watch the people and ducks on the lake by the famous boathouse. It seemed like a great idea until I got there and saw all the tourists. Yea, they just ruined it with their loudness and camera flashes. Plus, street performers were showing up to try to woo money away from the tourists before some bridal party showed up for photos and shooed everyone away. I didn't even wait for it to come to that point to drive me away.

There was another smaller lake that would have to do. There was a couple benches on one side of the lake and a rather nice foot bridge that arched over the water. It was quiet and pretty much off anyone's radar, and it was vacant by the time I walked over. It was nice to just sit in peace and let the world just exist without me for a moment. But the silence let the emotions from finding Meghan dead, again, creep in and silent tears rolled down my cheeks.

I had tried to make things right. I tried and I had let her down. I tried at everything and maybe there was nothing I was good at. Maybe it was only having this ability – this power – that made me accomplish or do anything in life. I wrote a way to New York City, then struggled to get into college and to survive. So I wrote my acceptance into Columbia, then struggled to keep up my grades. I wrote myself higher test scores just like I wrote Meghan into my life when I couldn't take another shitty roommate.

My hand brushed away the tears that didn't run off my face fast enough. I didn't have time to mope or cry. I needed to keep going and... No. I had to give myself some time to deal with these emotions. *Ugh!* But it just felt like now wasn't the right time to do that.

I pulled out my notepad and a pen to make a list of things I needed. Other than location of a new place to live, I had to stick to just the basics. Graduation was only a couple months away and I really wanted to make it to the end just to prove to myself now that I, Haley Brown, could actually do something on my own. The college was probably going to check in on me to make sure I was doing alright with grieving over Meghan's death and probably send someone to counsel me on being the one to walk in and find her, and then about being attacked and almost murdered too.

I drew a bullet dot on the first line so I knew this was a list and didn't accidentally write something like I had done with Jen. I needed a monthly MetroCard for the subway, a complete and new wardrobe, a stocked fridge, a furnished apartment or loft, a laptop computer, and the textbooks and supplies that I would need to help me finish out the year. Some cash would be nice until I got a job. I should probably write off my cell phone bill too by making a loophole in the system or maybe removing my account information from their system but still making a way for me to go undetected while having service. Yea, that last one sounded the best for flying under the radar and stopping some evil genius from tracking me down using my phone number.

Now it just left the question of where I would live. I was a broke college student, swimming in debt. That was even before I lost everything when I lost my best friend. The campus housing was, and always had been, completely full. Finding a place in the Upper West Side, or even the Upper East Side, would be nothing short of a miracle. Everyone wanted to be by the only green looking park in the city. And I didn't trust the Midtown landlords after horror stories that I heard over the years. That was always the place with the nicest people. My dream location had to be Murray Hill though. It was in the middle of everything and had a whole lot more to do... if I could actually motivate myself to be that outgoing person that left her apartment. Maybe West Village is where I should aim for. But, like for so many others, it was out of my reach right now. I'd find a place, for now, and graduate. Waiting a couple years, I'll let myself disappear from suspicion and then pounce on my dream home and start my dream life. But that still left the question of where a broke college girl would live.

Brooklyn.

It was a place I hadn't really spent much time in but people went on about it. It seemed the most reasonable option for my story. There had to be subway trains that were basically a straight shot – because after years of living here I still hadn't completely figured them out.

I turned sideways on the bench and set the notepad down in front of me. Leaning over slightly, I started to write about my new life. I explained how an unknown relative owned a small home just outside Williamsburg and agreed to rent it out to me for a small fee while they were gone south for the colder season. It was supposed to be convenient to public transportation that would take me back to Columbia, and it was also modestly furnished. I worked out how I had been there last weekend and stocked the fridge and moved in my new wardrobe, school supplies, and set up my new computer. That was also the reason why I had a monthly MetroCard in my wallet right now.

It would explain everything except where I was getting the money to keep this life. I knew that I was going to have to find a job right away. The strange part was that I had no idea what I wanted to do. Even college, it wasn't something I was entirely passionate about. It was what caused the least screw-ups in history. I just knew that I didn't want to work in fast food or as a lifeguard in some community pool, like I had back in high school. If I worked at Starbucks – my only true love it seemed – I'd probably spend my whole time drinking the coffee instead of serving it. But coffee was something that I knew pretty well. I'd leave that open as a possibility.

Getting a job where people gossiped or they continually ran the news would be the best for my current mission of revenge and salvation. Only place I could think about was at a gym or hair salon where there was always a television on or freely talking individuals.

Neither I could stand. It seemed Starbucks was back at the top of my short job list. A grocery store cashier was probably another easy gig that would give me access to newspapers and small talk. Probably wouldn't give me too much spending money though. I'd have to put in applications. It was as simple as that. And this time I was determined not to just write myself the job... even though I just wrote myself an entirely new life.

Tucking my notepad safely in the confines of my backpack and tossing the pen in on top, I got up and started to make my way out of the park. I need to complete and put in those applications today. I'd head back to my new home, get settled in, cry out all the emotions warring inside me, and then worry about... *crap.* I had a date tomorrow.

Crap!

Even more reason to get home and relax. It might be the only time I had to relax before the world exploded and – or – I graduated. Okay, melodramatic to the extreme but dating seemed scarier than murder right now. Probably because the two versions of me – the current one that just learned her roommate died and the one that knew her roommate was killed after leaving the coffee shop – were slowly merging emotions together and I was getting through things in my head faster. Yea, seeing Carter tomorrow was the thing I was worrying about the most. Especially after that kiss.

And why had he even kissed me? We were practically strangers. Unlike me, he didn't need a reason to play the ham and dream up something between us. Which made me remember how things were left off with his frat brother showing up. I hope Carter didn't get too much shit over it.

Carter was the thought that made my subway ride disappear. I was standing in front of a nice brownstone on a nice street in Brooklyn before I snapped out of my daydream haze. Somehow I had gotten to the point of wondering what he would look like with his shirt off. Maybe Meghan had been right all along. I should have tried dating again. Maybe the thing with Carter was just pent up emotions and missed opportunities that now were laid out in front of me. I could take a chance with this guy or just write myself emotionally dead inside. Well, at least towards love and romance. Maybe make myself a nun too while I was at it...

It was quiet inside the new place. Clean and neatly organized. I really would have liked to meet this "relative" person I was renting from just so they could explain their décor preferences and how they made everything so functional and organized. Okay, maybe it was slightly craving a little mess and noise in this solemn place. I was so used to having a roommate or my sister around. It was going to take some time to adjust.

I set my backpack down by the door and locked myself in before going to explore. I wanted to make sure everything was set just like how I wrote it. I didn't exactly want any surprises, and I wanted to make sure I had everything before my thinking side of my brain shut off for the night. And it was close. I saw what was to be my bed and there was a strong pull to try it out. I knew if I sat down on it, then I'd want to lay out on the lush comforter. Then I'd be snoozing in dreamland and probably drooling on the pillow in five minutes. But it looked so enticing...

I jumped as my cell phone vibrated. It felt like my heart was going to beat out of my chest. Who the hell was texting me at a time like this? Sure, I wanted the deterrent from laying down and passing out. I just didn't want it to also have given me a heart attack. I glanced down at the lock screen.

Carter "Sexypants" Hathorn

Sexypants? Crap...

I hadn't looked down to be a perv on his groin nor had I really took a look at his butt as he led me back up to his room. Missed chances that now bothered me. It probably should have been his moment of arrogance when he added himself to my contact list, but it wasn't really. It was almost... cute.

Carter: Can u dance?

Can I dance? That was kind of a strange question. Was his big date idea really nothing more than taking me to a club and feeding me alcoholic drinks all night? That didn't seem like what he asked me to do earlier.

Me: Define dance

Carter: Shakin ur booty

Okay, that still wasn't entirely clear. I wonder if Carter was going to be able to give the answer I was fishing for. I could just ask him to tell me the name of the place he wanted to go and then run an internet search for it. That way I would know exactly what I was getting myself into, but it would ruin the surprise and bit of excitement over not knowing.

Me: Grinding the club or like slow dancing?

He suddenly seemed like he was taking his time. He'd replied almost instantly just a minute ago. What could have happened? Did anything happen? Maybe Carter just got tired of me asking him a question about his question. Maybe he realized that I just wasn't worth it or that if the plan was to take me to a club that I was less likely to willingly go. He could be cutting his losses.

Carter: *Don't put that in my head*

I swallowed hard when his text finally came through. Glancing at what I had sent him, I could figure out what happened. His mind had probably pictured it and he had needed a moment before trying to talk to me again. At least it wasn't longer than what it was. I did *not* want to know if I had caused an impromptu hand session. I was about to text him back that I was sorry, when another one of his texts came through.

Carter: *Swing dancing*

Swing dancing... Was this some weird *Footloose* alternate dimension? I didn't know anyone still swing danced, much let a frat guy with a huge porn collection that hit the gym probably fairly regularly.

Carter: *?*

Taking a deep breath, I tried to figure out what I should text and what I shouldn't. It was a slippery slope that I realized I had gotten myself into. This was, technically, writing. I hadn't danced before in my life. Not unless you count the slow song dancing back at the high school prom, but that was just getting as close as you could and swaying back and forth. If I said I could, then he might ask who taught me or where I learned some move if my writing powers took the small "yes" and had

131

a field day. The interesting part was that Carter was suggesting something I could actually choose to experience for the first time. I could even be a little flirty with it too.

Me: Never did that. You willing to teach me?

Carter: Be my honor Melony

Carter: be my honor m'lady

Carter: srry autocorrect

Who the hell was Melony? I could understand it was a typing error but now it teased my thoughts and tormented me – something I didn't want to admit. There were two choices here that I saw. One, I could take the higher road and accept that it was simply a mistake that his phone's autocorrect made to girl's name that, maybe by his operating system or Google, was commonly popular. Or two, I could...

Me: Who's Melony?

Yep. Two was taking the low road and just asking him who that girl was and if he was seeing her on the side. Maybe he was a douchebag and had a girlfriend but was trying to get something, anything, from me behind her back. I was not – not now and not ever – going to be some side chick sneaking around with a guy.

Carter: My sis

Wow. That deflated my anger fast. Now I felt a little guilty for jumping to conclusions. I really had no right to. I just met Carter and we didn't really know each other. His room gave me no indication to jump to the conclusions that I had. I was in the wrong here.

Me: Sorry

Carter: Me too. She's a pain

132

Me: No, I thought she was your girlfriend or something...

Back to silence. This wasn't good. I shouldn't have admitted that. That was opening mouth and inserting foot. It probably just screwed things up completely between us. The odd thing was that I was slowly realizing how much I actually wanted something to happen between Carter and me. Okay, not jumping in bed right away, but casually talking to each other or dating. I actually didn't want to mess this up and lose him. It was so strange. The only thing I could blame was that kiss, and that was his doing. Okay, I blamed Carter. This was all his fault, and now I was caring and worrying.

Carter: If I had one I wouldnt have ask u or kissd u

Now he must have thought the worst about me. Because I knew it didn't take a blind man to see that that's what I had thought he was doing.

Me: That's why I said I was sorry.

Carter: Iam single

Me: I know that now.

Carter: lol cos I'm just saying :P

Me: Okay, okay... my bad. So this swing dancing thing?

Carter: Mhmm what about tit?

Oh, he was horrible at texting or typing or maybe just English in general. I knew I was slightly more grammatically inclined, but still... could he not read the words he was writing? Tit. Iam. Kissd. He was lucky I was – well, could make myself – a genius. I know I shouldn't be making assumptions, but let's just pretend he has big thumbs and they hit all the buttons on the screen.

Me: So we're going and you're going to teach me?

It took a while before he responded.

What was he doing? I knew that I shouldn't care, but part of me wanted to know. I needed to picture what he was up to and where he was and what he was wearing and... *Oh. My. God.* I was getting obsessed with him. Carter wasn't even a crush! Okay, maybe he was a little. Ugh, I felt like such a girl...

And I kind of liked that.

It had been a long time since I felt this kind of free with someone. It was way too soon to have any kind of real connection to this guy, but there was a chance that something could be there.

Carter: Maybe lol

Somehow he was both irritating and adorable... I wasn't sure how I actually felt about it. When my eyes saw the time stamp on his latest message, I realized that I had killed a lot of time just sitting here talking to a boy. At that moment, my stomach decided to grumble and remind me that I had wasted a lot of time and my hunger needed to be sated.

Me: Text me where, when and if then. Gotta go make dinner.

Carter: Mhmm. What ya having?

Now it was my turn to be adorably irritating. Well, maybe it was just flirty.

Me: Food

And I just left him with that. I plugged my phone into the wall outlet by my bed and left the phone there to change while I headed to the kitchen. Sure, he might get a little frustrated when I don't reply instantly. But Carter would logically know I wasn't going to be attached to my phone while playing around in a kitchen with knives and pans and fire and stuff. Okay, well, maybe it was a little bit of payback for what he'd done. It wasn't that big of a mind game…

Chapter Seven

I glanced at the time on my phone yet again. Carter was late. He had said to meet him at the corner of Nicholas Avenue and West 124th Street at noon. It was already quarter after, and still no sign of him.

I should have known that I was going to be set up. Last night I had gotten a little carried away and probably teased a little too much. Maybe his frat house had another party and he found a better girl to spend his time on. Okay, by better, I mean his brother set him up with some random – probably drunk – chick and he got laid last night. He probably thought she was prettier too.

It felt like I was making too many assumptions about the guy, but I just couldn't shake it. That was what guys did, right? I should just go back home and try to deal with school and cramming for the classes I was going to struggle with now that I banned myself from writing out passing grades.

Maybe I should give Carter one last chance. What was the worst that could happen? Have a girl answer his phone and laugh at me. Yea, that was probably the worst but I thought that I could handle it. I pulled out my phone and hit his name. The dial tone rang in my ear as I waited for him to pick up. Someone nearby had an annoying ringtone going off that almost sounded like...

"Hello?"

Okay, so it wasn't some random girl answering his phone. But that didn't explain why he wasn't here.

"It's Haley. I thought we were meeting up today at noon."

"We are. I'm there right now, waiting for you."

What? How was that possible? I looked up and down the street. Carter definitely wasn't here. I know I shouldn't assume things, but maybe he was running late and saying that was his way of trying to buy himself some time to get here.

"Carter, I'm at the corner. I've been here for twenty minutes and haven't seen you. If you –"

"Wait a minute." He just cut me off and then told me to wait?

The other end of this phone call was all silence. I had my coffee this morning, so I know I wasn't just being irritable. This was all him and how he was playing around with his game and...

"Found you." It wasn't the voice on the other end of the phone I heard.

I glanced to my left and saw his head was poked around the corner of the building. Oh. My. God. I felt stupid. My shoulders drooped as I walked over to meet him.

"You were just around the corner," I groaned. "How long were you standing there?"

137

Of course he chuckled as he pulled me into a bear hug. "Just for about fifteen minutes. I didn't get here much before noon."

Well, at least there was that. I didn't feel too guilty with him having shown up after me. Now, if he'd been standing here and I had walked passed him, I would felt like a horrible person. He would have been a horrible person too if he had just walked right by me too, but it seemed like we had come from two different directions and stopped at two different corners. Somehow we both were right and both were wrong.

"So... you still want to do whatever we were doing and just forget all about this?"

Carter chuckled. "No. I'd rather not forget anything with you, Haley. How about I just promise not to hold it against you and to never bring it up again? If I do, I'll let you punch my arm."

Somehow I feel like that's more of a punishment for me. There was plenty of muscle on his arms and I wasn't exactly a body builder. I'd probably break my hand if I punched him. Maybe I should just forget about that comment too and not hold that against him.

"Sounds like a deal." I glanced around, trying to figure out where this swing dance place was. "So where is this place?"

"Right to the point, huh?" He smiled and held out his hand. "Come on, it's just a couple blocks away but we're stopping at this awesome food cart first."

Food cart? Like not a food truck? I knew the food carts around the city were usually vendors ripping off tourists with outrageous prices for roasted nuts, kababs, and hotdogs. I'd be okay with a hotdog or kabab, but the quality really was more miss than hit with those places. That and, if this was a real date, you'd think that someone wouldn't want to try and poison someone they were trying to get with. Maybe that was just my opinion. At least with a food truck, it was like a mini kitchen on wheels that had a better reputation... and more choices.

"A food cart," I said deadpanned. It seemed like he wasn't going to budge or explain more until I took his hand. So I did. I took his hand and he started to lead me down the street. His hand felt oddly nice and warm...

Carter laughed and it almost infected me and got me laughing too. That was until I remembered why he was laughing. I had just pointed out that he said we were going to a food cart. Maybe – because he was a frat guy – he thought that was a great date and the only thing to make it a better date was if there was a cold beer with it... and sex at the end of the date.

"Haley, when you get a load of this food cart, you'll be eating those words. I would literally eat every meal here if it wasn't so far away from the house."

"It's probably like three bus stops away." That wasn't far at all. "The subway probably comes right along here."

Actually, that part I knew. I had taken the subway back over from Brooklyn. After getting off, it was only a two block walk to get to the corner where we were meeting up. I just had to ask, even though there was a risk of being laughed at again.

"How is that far from your house at all?"

Carter didn't exactly laugh, but he did give me a sideways glance that said I was crazy. "It's more than a block walk. I ain't got time or energy for that."

I wanted to ask him what he did have time and energy for. I mean, honestly, he had to spend it at the gym to get muscles like that, and walking was just the same as working out. Exercise was exercise. He really was the stereotypical frat boy. Did he not realize that?

"You know walking is just exercise, right?" I looked up at him and watched as a slow smile grew on his face.

"Yea, I know, but it's not the same. I could do a lot of walking but not burn any fat off or work up a sweat. I wouldn't be pushing my body and wearing myself out. And if I'm good to think afterwards then it wasn't a good workout. I need something that would basically kill me for the day."

I didn't want to point out how those last words were really the wrong kind of thing to be saying. After all, someone from Columbia just died, whether he knew it or not. But if I said that, Carter might realize who I was and he might have heard who my roommate was. I didn't really want him to feel guilty and end up treating me like a fragile little baby after that. Besides, I would just come off sounding like I was dissing his workout preferences and like I had no idea how working out or exercise actually worked for the human body.

Which I didn't know.

"You don't have any fat to work off," I said instead. Falling into an awkward silence was more terrifying than letting what we had going on just die because I said something stupid.

Carter chuckled but beamed a smile my way. "Thanks, Haley. I really try to stay fit." He lifted our joined hands to point somewhere off to my side. "Working it off so hard means that I can eat anything and everything that I want. And that's the food cart over there."

I took the two second distraction in his pace to look over my shoulder. It wasn't what I expected. Carter gave me a little tug and walked me over to the nicest looking food cart I had ever seen. It definitely wasn't peanuts and it wasn't some mystery meat on a stick or in a bun either.

"It smells *really* good." And we were still a block and a half away. That *never* happened with street food before. "What is this place?" I asked in awe.

Carter didn't laugh this time. "It's Ben's Pizzazz."

We got in the decently long line for the food cart. Ben's Pizzazz. It wasn't exactly that descriptive. At least as far as what kind of food was being served. It made me think that everything was going to have confetti or glitter or some pointless extra thing to give it that pizzazz. Or maybe the cooking vendor put on a show in the way that some expert bartenders added flare to how they mixed up drinks.

"So what exactly does this place have?" I asked but then instantly thought better. I had to be more on my game when I was around Carter it seemed like. "I'm talking about what kind of food I can expect here, Carter, before you twist my words."

"Moi?" He actually tried to look innocent. Psh, like he was innocent. Carter seemed to realize that I wasn't taking the bait.

"Ben's is the best pizza around. It's a little unconventional for a food cart to have pizza. You know, 'cos food trucks have the space for ovens and stuff. But this guy actually figured out this great way to make a pizza crust on like the thing they make crepes on, but only he gets this fire oven action on it too. It's hard to explain unless you see him working it in action. Other than that, he's got these hot griddle sandwiches. I got this hot shredded turkey and ham one time and it was banging."

It was a bit hypnotizing to watch him talk about food. Either he just loved food or he really loved this place. That wasn't a bad thing. It was just another thing that I didn't really expect from Carter. It seemed like I was assuming a lot of things about him, and it was starting to make me feel guilty.

"So what are you going to get?"

He took a moment and really seemed to be thinking it over. "I think I'll get a pizza if you're up with sharing with me. Then you can see how he does it."

"I guess that depends." I gave him a moment to stew, which he did not fail me and asked what it depended on. "Do you put weird toppings on your pizza like pineapple or mushrooms or," I faked a gasp, "sausage with bacon?"

Carter laughed and we moved up in the line to be next. "First, what's wrong with a sausage and bacon pizza? Bacon is the shit."

"You have sausage that's basically meat chunks and then you add bacon that's small meat chunks, only cruncher and that could chip a tooth or something."

"Right," he teased. "So you good with sharing with me if I get pepperoni with green peppers and truffles?"

Okay, did he not hear me a moment ago? Unless I'm wrong, truffles are a type of mushroom. Did he think he was pulling a fast one on me just because they were a fancy ingredient?

"Is that a trick question?"

"No... why?" He seemed puzzled.

Okay, he genuinely didn't seem like he was playing around. "Truffles are a type of mushroom. Well, they're a fungus but still."

He was quiet as the person in front of us ordered and then stepped aside. We were up next and I could see how fancy the menu actually was. Truffles wasn't just the only thing that set this food cart apart from the others. There was a grilled avocado BLT sandwich with arugula. Pasta even made an appearance on the menu, and how it worked in a food cart was a mystery to me.

"What can I get ya?"

And now it was our turn.

Carter was looking at me, waiting for me to either shoot him down and cause the other patrons in line to riot against us for taking so long or to give in and accept the fancy mushrooms. It came down to the real beef I had with mushrooms... and that was that they smelled weird. I've been tricked before and ate them, which weren't too horrible. Maybe these truffles would actually taste okay.

"I'll split the pizza with you," I grumbled.

"You sure?" Carter asked. I nodded and he placed the order with the food cart man, paying him as well. Carter ushered me aside with him to stand on the side of the cart. "Okay, now watch."

He pointed to a slowly turning flat stone. "That's the crepe maker looking thing I was talking about. So first, he cuts off a chunk of dough from the large glob under the cart there. Forms it like that and spreads it out on the stone."

I watched as the vendor did just that and then took a moment to take another order. It was one of those avocado BLT sandwiches. While our crust set and started baking, the vendor tossed green slices on the griddle portion of his cart while fresh cooking bacon filled the air. It was a little mesmerizing to watch this man move from that back to our pizza to flip the dough that was just starting to turn golden brown on that side. It went back to spinning while the man put the finishing touches on the sandwich. Finally, he went back to add the sauce and toppings. Then he flipped down a top portion from an arm to brown the top. It reminded me of the special chairs in hair salons were ladies would sit and wait for their perms or hair colorings to set beneath that dome top.

"And now he's just melting the cheese and basically toasting the top."

Had Carter been explaining things this whole time? I seriously just zoned out. I hope that he didn't realize it or get upset about it. It wasn't like I did it on purpose, but this food cart guy was just too hard to look away from.

"Pepperoni, pepper, truffle pizza," the vendor called out.

Carter went over to grab the pizza and it seemed like he asked for it to be split because the man cut it in half and handed over two paper plates.

"Let's go sit over there." He nodded towards a low stone wall outside a building that portioned it off from the sidewalk. Sure, the building owners might not like people sitting on it but it wasn't like we were homeless or there to trash it.

He handed me a plate with the two large slices. "Bon appétit," were two words that Carter barely squeezed out before taking a bite.

Shrugging it off, I followed suit. I see why he couldn't wait. This tasted amazing – mushrooms and all. I think I was more stunned at that than Carter was at how I didn't hesitate to eat. He was probably used to girls that nibbled at a salad and then only ate half a leaf. I was enjoying this pizza.

"Good?" He asked, teasing. I just nodded my answer and he laughed. "Even with the mushrooms?"

Oh, he definitely wasn't going to let me forget that I made one concession as to what couldn't be on the pizza... then was devouring it. It was hard to make an effective defense case when it was just too good with the truffle shavings on top to really complain.

"Yes," I mumbled quietly.

I really hoped that he hadn't heard me, but he did. Carter didn't take a jab at me though. Maybe he was smart enough to realize that our level of teasing was getting to the point where there might be a limit, for me, and that he might cost himself the chance at another date if he crossed it. Wait. Why was I thinking about the possibility of a second date? Crap, I was starting to like this guy even though he was testing me.

We finished our halves of the pizza in silence and then Carter collected the paper plates and charted them off to the recycling bin. He walked back over and held out his hand again.

"Shall we?"

I reached out and took his hand. This did feel like more than just a date, with how he was acting and going over the top. But maybe that was just because I lacked experience. Maybe I should just be going through the motions and take cues from Carter. Well, at least until he tried to get in my pants or something.

Carter led me another block or so from the food cart to a normal looking brick building. He held the door open for me and we headed inside. That was when I heard it. There was some kind of upbeat music playing and it made my feet want to dance. Well, it gave me that urge to dance. Of course, Carter was going to have to teach me how but that was a minor technicality. Hopefully he was a decent enough teacher; otherwise, I was going to have to sneak off to the bathroom and write myself some dance skills.

"So do you want stand in the hallway a moment and have me teach you or are you fine with other people being around?" Carter stopped outside one of the two large dance rooms.

I got what he was asking. He was asking if I was okay with other people watching and possibly judging me for not knowing how to dance or if I would rather him protect my ego and go over the steps out here. It was really considerate of him, and the fact that he thought of it meant a lot. But I knew that chances were that I wouldn't be coming back here. There was a room full of people that I'd never see again, even if I befriended them, because the fact was that this was New York City – population a zillion.

"Maybe just show me a couple steps out here? All that fancy stuff you can teach me in there where you can get the brownie points for being a hot teacher."

Crap! I didn't mean to blurt out that last part. Now he knew that I thought he was hot. I didn't even want to accept that he really was hot half the time, and that was just to myself. Now I just admitted it to a frat guy with an ego probably the size of a semi-truck.

"I think you're pretty hot too." He smiled a bit and seemed to be more at ease. "I'll show you the basic steps out here and that's all. I don't think I can trust getting too close to you without eyes around."

That should have been a red flag to back out of this. Seeing as I had just fought off a man trying to murder me a couple days ago; although, I think I could handle one trying to kiss or grope me in the hallway.

I nodded and he moved to stand next to me. Asking me to follow his moves and mirror him, Carter took me through the basic steps of swing dancing. It wasn't as awkward as I thought, seeing as we could hear the music bleeding out to where we lurked outside the doors. It was just more private and intimate than I would have thought. Yet, I still didn't want to run away. Not completely, at least.

"Are you ready to try dancing with me?"

Carter had stayed beside me and made sure that I got the easy basic steps down. I knew that's not how dancing was done. He needed to be in front of me and probably holding my hand or touching me somehow. That's the part that made my stomach flutter and kicked up the nerves.

I couldn't trust myself to say a word and instead just nodded. He covered one of my hands with his, moving it to rest on his shoulder. He took my other hand in his while he rested his free one on my hip. Carter took the first move and I followed, rather delayed, in his wake. It wasn't that I forgot the simple steps in the last two minutes. It was that being this close to him was just affecting me, and it didn't help that I knew he actually liked me in return. It made me wonder for a moment what that mutual attraction might cause later tonight. Would Carter be so bold as to try and lock lips... again?

"That's it, Haley. You really got this." There was a reassuring smile on his face. I highly doubted that I was good enough right now to warrant that kind of praise. "Let's head inside."

And there it was. That inkling of dread creeping back in. I was going to have to go into a room full of people and dance with a guy that I could barely keep myself together around. I wasn't worried about people laughing at my poor dance moves; I was worried they'd laugh at me for drooling over my partner. Yea, it even sounded stupid and embarrassing. I should tell Carter that I wasn't ready to buy some time to get over him, but he already had the door opened to the room and was leading me inside.

There were quite a few dancing couples going at it. Some were doing the same thing which I took to be basic, normal swing, while others were doing twists and flips. And my stomach was joining them. I didn't expect to be twisted and spun around. Carter didn't go over any of that. What if he wanted to do that with me?

He seemed to sense my hesitation and glanced across the room at what had caught my attention. "Don't worry, Haley, I won't be doing any of that with you. That's more like second date kind of stuff."

And there was that smile again. I know I could have corrected him and said that a second date was so far out of the question or still yet to be earn or that he couldn't talk about that when we hadn't even finished the first. But I wasn't kidding anyone, let alone myself. I'd give him another shot... if he wanted to give me another shot.

The dancing wasn't really the hard part once we got going. It ended up being my inability to not stare at Carter, because he already caught me twice and he was getting that cocky smile that accompanied his teasing words. When I struggled to avoid looking at him, he'd start making small talk. By the end of the two hour session, we gotten into deeper territory like hobbies, likes and dislikes, and embarrassing stories...

"Excuse me, but is Haley Brown here?"

Everyone stopped when the two police officers entered and shouted. The music quickly cut out once it was realized there were there for someone. Well, there for me.

"Is Haley Brown here?" The tanner officer asked again. Surely we all would hear the question now that there was no music.

Part of me was just waiting for someone to rat me out, but then I realized that Carter was the only one who knew my name. Well, just my first name. He hadn't even moved a muscle. Not to look at me. Not to nudge me forward. Not to point me out. I wanted to know what he was thinking right now, but I also didn't. I knew that this was about Meghan's murder and I could guess that they tracked my phone. I just didn't know why they needed to come pick me up again.

I stepped towards them. "I'm Haley Brown."

What if they were here to bring me to another interrogation? Oh, I did not want to have to retell the details again. To me, there were two separate stories about how Meghan was killed... but to them, there was only one. I had to focus and make sure I didn't slip and mix up the details. I couldn't do that while Carter was here being eye candy. On the other hand, if they were here to arrest me then I wouldn't have to worry about kissing Carter tonight or calling him back after the mandated two day grace period or waiting for him to call me or even about the possibility of there being a second date. That kind of bummed me out.

"Ms. Brown, we need you to come to the precinct with us."

I just nodded and complied. They hadn't handcuffed me... yet. That had to be a good sign. It was probably the only good sign I had right now. If I glanced back at

Carter, I probably wouldn't see anything I'd want to. I definitely wouldn't hear or see him again.

It had been another round of questioning, but this time from Meghan's parents. They wanted to know what happened, but it wasn't like I could tell them all the bloody and gory details. I told them what the cops glazed over – someone broke into our apartment, stabbed Meghan, and then tried to kill me. I could tell them that I didn't think it was a robbery. I could tell them that we didn't see anyone lurking around or following us. I could lie and say neither of us were threatened. It seemed to give them a little piece of mind to think that this was a freak accident for Meghan, but at least justice had been served for her.

I couldn't let them know the truth and have them hate me for being the reason she was gone. For once, I actually liked having someone be concerned for me and my safety... after I slipped and mentioned the guy I shot said he had a partner. That was something the cops heard as well, from the other side of the glass wall, and now were looking into. Guess the plus side was that either the police or I were going to find the other person behind this first. I was betting on me.

It was after nine o'clock by the time I made it home. The house was dark as I walked up the few steps on my stoop and let myself in. The quiet was a relief after having to deal with reality again. That was until after I had made dinner, showered, and was lying in bed trying to will myself asleep. I reached over to check the time on my phone and realized there was a text message there. A text message from Carter...

The problem with reading it was knowing that it wasn't going to be good. Maybe he was the polite kind of guy and was gently turning me down by saying it was nice to meet me but that we just wouldn't work out or I just wasn't what he was looking for. After the day I had being interrogated again, I don't think I really want to add the sting of rejection.

The best thing for me to do was – ignore what the cops said – and shut off my phone for the night. Then, tomorrow, I'd hunt for a job until my junker could deliver on those newspapers. While I could just leave my phone on – playing nice with the cops – and look for criminals that way, I didn't want any way for anyone to trace this back to me. What I learned from this whole ordeal was that there's a bottom line, a common denominator, and you did not want to be that. Marshall was going to come through for me, whether I wrote it or not.

Chapter Eight

He was there waiting for me when I got to 105th Street. It seemed that Marshall still was uneasy about doing business with a woman, or maybe he was fearing retribution from his last buyer. I knew it wasn't because my clothes were blood soaked last time we talked. Maybe he was scoping out places to eat, seeing as that had been our deal the last time we spoke.

He had a shopping cart with a nice large stack and even attempted to smile when he spotted me. "I wasn't sure if you'd still be interested in me and my papers," he meekly spoke.

"I'm still interested and, even if I wasn't, I would have still shown up to make good on our deal. You spoke to me the other day, and I owe you a good meal for that." And there'd be more meals in it for him if Marshall could keep producing papers that helped me get Meghan's killers.

I leaned over to take a peek in the cart. He was a rather organized man, which meant these papers were going to be in nice condition. But the simple act was really to show him that I was interested and that I was taking this contract seriously by evaluating him. It has come to be expected by the homeless that they would be judged.

"What was your last buyer's pay arrangement?" If I thought that Marshall was nervous before, he certainly was nervous now. Either he was embarrassed to tell me their arrangement or trying to think of how to convince me of a lie.

"Each stack he gave me five dollars for. Paid upon delivery and inspection."

Sounded like a miserable truth. Marshall would collect everything he could only to have his buyer throw out half of his stacks and then pay for whatever he wanted. It didn't sound right to me and maybe Marshall's nervousness was over worrying that I'd want a contract like that. And five dollars for a foot or two-foot high stack seemed low. This guy couldn't live off that. Begging almost pulled in more. Then again, paper didn't have a large market like cans or lost goods did.

I could barter or accept Marshall's last rate to save a nickel, but it meant nothing when I could write. "I'll pay you double for each stack you bring. If you run short or come back with nothing, I'll still pay you two dollars for your trouble. Pay will be upon delivery and I feel no need to inspect your papers. You seem honest and your cart is clean."

If I didn't know better, I'd say Marshall was choking up. I was either a godsend or a hoax in his book. Add in the fact he was getting a meal on top of this and he probably didn't believe a word. So I dug into my purse and pulled out a ten dollar bill. He took it, but just stared at it like it wasn't real.

"I'll be taking what you have today, but first lunch." His gaze came up to meet mine. Looked like he was starting to believe this was real. "Whatever you want. It's on me."

His eyes drifted pass me as he judged the cost of restaurants and food carts. I knew he was trying to pick the cheapest just to keep from ruining the chances of keeping a long contract. That hadn't been my intent.

"How about we order a couple pizzas? I'm a college student." Or, well, technically I was for a few weeks longer and it fit a certain stereotype. "You can take all the leftovers. I have a box of ramen to eat later so I won't be hungry."

"Yea. Yea, sounds good." Marshall nodded along.

The problem was in the ordering and the wait. I doubted he wanted to wait around for twenty or thirty minutes for a couple pizza pies to be whipped up. And I couldn't take this guy back to the food stand that Carter had taken me too. Mostly because I was irrationally worried about running into the guy. A guy that probably never wanted to see me again. And now that unread text message felt ten times heavier in my pocket.

"Well, to get something fast, there's Little Caesars. They're supposed to have pizzas ready to grab and go. Are you okay with cheese, pepperoni, or sausage?"

Again, I got a nod. I had to press him a little to get a word out about what he liked – pepperoni. It seemed like things would be easy. While I loved pepperoni, especially with mushrooms and green peppers, I was going to order cheese. Marshall needed something else and it would get boring to eat the same thing, at least I think so, and sausage just feels weird to eat on pizza.

We walked, mostly in silence, towards the nearest location that showed up on my phone. All I could hear were the constant sounds of traffic and the clinging wheels on his shopping cart. I knew that this was an odd arrangement, but it was one that I had to make. I had just tucked my phone in my back pocket when it started to ring.

"Shouldn't you get that, miss?"

Marshall was a gentleman, at least to me now. I could show him the same respect. "It would be rude to answer it while we're getting lunch. I'm sure if it's important that they'll call back later."

Or it was the police and they'd just end up tracking my cell phone… again.

Or was it Carter and pigs were flying.

Inside the store, it smelled hot and tomato-y. Being the middle of the day, there were enough people pushing around in front of the counter and some trying to get to the few bar-style tables around the walls to quickly eat their slice before running back to the office. I noticed that Marshall hadn't entered with me. I wanted to brush it off as if he thought it was too crowded and knew I could handle it alone, but I knew it was only because he was a second-class citizen. Even with me – a paying customer – I'm sure the manager would have thrown him out.

He was watching me from the very far side of the window storefront. I could pretend that he's just watching the cart to make sure my papers and his goods

157

aren't stolen, instead of thinking that he's only watching to see if I keep up my end of the bargain. When the crowd clears out in front of me, I place my order and a few bills on the counter before the hot pies get shoved in my hands so I can move for the next hungry executive or starving college kid.

"It's crazy in there," I commented, trying to sound casual about it and dispel some tension, on my way out. It's because I've been in his shoes that I want to try to make him comfortable and set him at ease. I don't think I'm really doing that. "Do you want to head the park and find someplace to sit and eat?"

I was hauling this man all over the city, probably. It was only a few blocks to Central Park, and I'm sure that's about where he was sleeping. It was a rough place to camp due to vandals and police, but it was also more hidden than hiding on a stoop to catch some Z's. Then again, it was another bunch of assumptions that I was making.

Marshall nodded and followed after me. It was like he didn't have a choice, and maybe that's how he felt. I was the one with the money. I was the one making this contract. I was even the one holding the pizzas. I really needed to ignore the differences between Marshall and me more. It was only going to make him more uncomfortable if I tried to compensate; that much I was realizing now.

I let him pick out a spot on the grass where he could maneuver his cart. I sat down across from him and opened the pizza boxes between us. He restrained himself to taking a single slice, but his eyes had doubled in size when he saw the melty cheesy goodness. There was no doubt in my mind that he wanted to devour every slice then and there, but this was also probably the only real meal that he's had in a while. He'd probably ration it for a few days instead.

I took a single slice of the cheese and quietly ate beside him. My eyes kept drifting back to the stack of papers. This was the way to bring Meghan's killers to real justice. This was the right path for me to take. I could feel it. Knowing the answer was just a couple feet away from me made me antsy to get back home and scour the worn pages. It was manners that kept me sitting on the grass with Marshall. I'd finish my slice and then excuse myself.

"It's almost time for my class." I got up and brushed off my ass. "I want to thank you for accepting my contract. I'll just take the papers and be going."

Marshall just nodded as he shoved the rest of his second slice in his mouth. I took that as permission to enter his cart.

The stack was heavy and I regretted not bringing a bag for them. There were none in Marshall's cart, even if I had wanted to impose. I just cradled the damp-smelling papers in my arms against my chest, just like I had always done with my high school textbooks. Without a second glance at my junker, I headed towards the subway. I couldn't wait to see who was in these papers, and to drop them. My arms were already starting to ache; and by the time I made it home, my muscles were burning and my nerves were fried. My phone kept ringing. I had tried to answer it once and nearly lost my stack of papers in the gap between the platform and the subway train. I don't know who was after me now, but they were going to hear it the second I dropped these papers.

They landed with a loud thud on the floor next to the table. I'll sit there later and go through them. But, for now, I needed to see who was blowing up my phone. The screen lit up with a whole list of text message previews and missed call notifications and bubbles informing me that I had voicemails waiting. There was just one name that popped out.

Carter.

Everything was from him. Was he really that desperate to dump me in person or, at least, in person over the phone? I unlocked the screen without glancing at the message previews.

Carter: u OK?
Carter: Call me wen u get this
Carter: Im worried. Haley cal
Carter: call me.
Carter: whats wrong?
Carter: Plz pick up ur phone
Carter: txt me ur ok, plz?

It seemed like he genuinely was worried about me. I kept reading the rest of the text messages; all were some degree of worry and begging. In one he got upset that I was ignoring him, but then apologized in the next. This wasn't what I expected at all. He wasn't supposed to care or worry about me. He was supposed to run for the hills. Didn't he know who I am? Well... I guess that never really came up.

"Hi, my name is Haley. And I killed my boyfriend and then was the reason my best friend was stabbed to death. Nice to meet you!"

I was about to toss the phone on the table to forget it for a while after this new revelation when it started ringing. His name popped up and my thumb accidentally brushed against the phone screen as I was putting it aside.

"Oh my god, Haley! You're alive. You picked up. You okay?" He spoke so fast. It was like he thought I'd hang up in a minute and he had to try to get everything said by then. "Wait... Haley, it is you, right?"

For a second maybe he thought I was my own murderer answering the phone. Not that Carter would know that I'd gotten a call like that. My mind needed to get off Meghan for a second. "Yea, it's me."

"God, I've been fucking worried. The cops just took off with you and I haven't heard a word since. I was thinking it was something bad and they like threw you in jail or something."

"Carter, I..." *I can't talk to you anymore. Go find a nice girl.*

But he pushed on. "I need to see you and know that you're ok."

My head was shaking, as if he could see me. "I don't think that's a good idea."

I didn't want him to think there was anything between us. Going to see him would mean that there was. Inviting him over meant Carter would know where I lived, and he could always come back...

"Haley, if you do not tell me where you live, I'll just call the cops and have them tell me. I don't know what you're so afraid of. I just want to make sure you're okay."

"Carter," I cut him off. "You have no idea what you're talking about. Okay? Cops talk to people all the time. Maybe I just had a parking ticket."

"I know about your roommate, Meghan. And you took the subway to our date; you don't drive. C'mon, Haley. What's the real reason?" He asked gently.

It knocked the wind out of me and I couldn't form a thought. Somehow he knew. Somehow he found out. There was just no way this was happening. If Carter was calling now, after knowing that, what did he really want?

"Haley, I'm sorry 'bout that. I'm guessing that's the reason you don't want to have me over. It's just that I like you and I'm worried about you. One of my frat brothers knew Meghan and what happened was terrible. I just want to be there for you so you know you're not alone."

A friend of Meghan's...

I didn't know who to trust, but hopefully being someone Meghan had trusted was worth something. I gave Carter my address and hung up. I didn't know if he'd come over after all or not. He knew what I had kept from him and he already had an impression of me after catching me at the frat house, having slept in his bed.

It took Carter almost forty minutes to get to my place. When I opened the door, he pulled me into his arms. I'm not going to lie – it felt nice. I probably held on longer than I should have, but he didn't say a thing when I finally stepped back and invited him inside. He just glanced around for a moment from the doorway.

"This is where you live?" He let out a whistle. "Don't know why you'd slum it in the dorms if you had this to come back to."

More like he was asking why I was Meghan's roommate on campus when we could have lived like queens out here. That hug almost tricked my brain to the point where I told him the truth. "A relative just took a trip and offered to let me stay here after what happened."

Carter nodded, accepting that as truth. He finally came in and, of course, the first thing he noticed was the one thing I couldn't really explain. "What's with the newspapers?"

I think at some point I had mentioned to him that my major was art history. Even if I hadn't, it would be best to play it safe and not equate the stack to homework. Could I pull it off as a personal interest piece? Art exhibit installation? Hobby? There were just too many follow-up questions that Carter could ask, and I probably wouldn't be able to keep everything straight.

"The guy that broke in said he was working with someone. I figured they're criminals or something. I thought maybe I could figure out who they are if I look at all the crime news. It's the only thing I can do now to help Meghan." That was the awful truth. I couldn't even use my power to help her.

"I think it's a good idea, Haley. Better than just sitting around waiting for them to find something."

No, it was a shitty idea. Looking at newspapers would lead to nothing but false leads and ink-smudged fingers. That's all it would lead to, unless the person looking was

163

me. Carter already knew about one secret; I couldn't let him know about the other.

"Let me help you look." Carter had his hands in his pant pockets, but shrugged the suggestion off like it was no big deal. "I know I don't know much about what happened, but you could tell me what I'm looking for." *No. No. No.* "Four eyes are better than two. Not to mention faster."

I shook my head. No. There was no way he was getting involved in this. Carter was going to walk out that door, forget my name, and... and he was giving me the sappy puppy-dog eyes?

"Pwease, Haley?"

Aw, shit...

"Fine," I grumbled, crossing my arms over my chest.

Carter leaned in to plant a kiss on my cheek. "You're not going to regret this."

He had the hugest shit-eating grin on his face as he stepped around me and took a seat at the table. I watched as he plucked a bunch off one of the stack and started to pick the newspapers apart into different sections. I don't know what dumbfounded me more: one, the fact that he was willingly to help; or two, that he kissed me. Sure it was a chaste kiss to the cheek, but it still was a kiss.

"Hey, you going to help or am I going to do all the work?" He joked.

And just like that, the spell was broken. One wise ass crack was all it was going to take with him, apparently. "Cork it, Carter."

Grumbling, I took the seat across from him and grabbed my own mini-stack. It seemed like he already had a system to split up the comics from the sports from the advertisements. It irked me a little that this "outsider" to my plans was doing so perfectly what I would have done... with my plans.

"You're making a cute grumpy face, Haley. Don't make me have to come over there and kiss a smile back on your face."

Shit.

It was tempting to stay pouting almost as much as it was to go over there and smack his arm. It just meant that I need to focus even more on jumping right in and getting started on finding these killers. I grabbed the newspaper on the top and started picking it apart and putting the different sections into the piles Carter had started. I tried my best not to look up over at him. Well, at least not too much. Carter was only focused on the newspapers. Occasionally he'd ask me if I thought something might fall into the pile of leads, but otherwise he sifted through his stack quietly. Meanwhile I chugged along slowly, having been staring at and zoning out over this hot guy that seemed to want to stick around to play with old newspapers.

Somehow, the sorting went by fast. It wasn't long before we had Marshall's stack reduced to a handful of pages and ripped out articles. By then, I had fixed us up some nachos and grabbed two cans of soda to help us power through the tough part of finding the killer. I tried to tell Carter enough of what I was looking for without making him concerned over what I might get myself or him into to by looking for the murderers and the worst of the worst. Chances were that these guys were low key enough that they wouldn't have gotten caught for murder, but they might have taken lesser charges to their names. Even describing the guy in my apartment to Carter had to be done cautiously. Carter was already protective of me – it seemed – and I didn't want his ego or jealousy taking over. Besides, who knew what was going through his mind right now?

The hours were starting to add up and we weren't getting any reliable leads. Most of the scraps of articles ended up in the trash with the rest of the sorted newspaper, minus the comics. Hey, I'm a sucker for a good laugh and I could really use one these days. Besides, there was a giant dog and an orange cat that I needed to get caught up on.

But it still boiled down to a fruitless night and I was getting tired. Besides, Carter still needed to make his way home. I didn't want it to get too late and strand him here when the subway shut down for the night, giving him a reason to stay. As much as I thought I'd want that, I was pretty sure that I wouldn't want that the next day. He could be a friend... well, a close friend. Fine, I could date him and we could go out but staying in would be too dangerous. Eventually one of us would make a move. My bet was him. Totally him. But probably me. Ugh, I felt like I just couldn't think around this guy.

"Oh, wow, it's getting pretty late." I pretended to stretch my back in an effort to tell him I was tired of sitting around. Then I realized that he probably saw it as me showing off my chest for him. *Gawd!* "I probably should let you go. You don't want to end up my slave, clipping newspapers."

He laughed and got up, stretching his own way that lifted his shirt to give me a peek of what was underneath. "I probably should get going. Got some calculus to try and bust out for tomorrow."

I watched Carter walk around the table and head towards the door. Of course, I was walking him out. And of course, I checked out his ass a little... Okay, maybe I really did like this guy.

"Hey, why don't you stop by the house tomorrow? I can round up all the junk papers we got laying around. There's a bunch of shit in the basement." Carter paused in the doorway. "This guy might have gotten caught and he won't be in the newer ones you got in that stack."

It was a glimmer of hope for a rather disappointing night of failed success. There had been no one convicted of anything close to murder or anyone sounding like the guy that attacked me. And it was also a way that I could see Carter again. I don't know what it was about him, but I really was liking him even though he pushed my buttons sometimes. At the frat house, we wouldn't be alone so it wouldn't get weird or... things wouldn't happen, let's say. Not that I was really worried about that. I was barely thinking about it. There was nothing that –

"So what ya say?"

Crap.

I had gotten lost in my head there for a moment. "Sure, I'll stop by after noon with what papers I have left. That way if there's nothing at your frat house, then we can still get something done." My face wasn't going to fit the smile I had growing. "*And* I won't have to deal with getting rid of these myself."

"Oh, I see. Just using me for my trash can." He shook his head and headed down the front steps, laughing. "See ya, Haley."

"Night, Carter."

Chapter Nine

I didn't think a frat house could be so quiet. It was suspicious. There was no way every brother was either in class or just out. Carter must have done something to arrange this alone time with me. Maybe his plan was to kill me. By the looks of it, this basement was crammed with junk and my body would easily be hidden behind a stack of totes or cardboard boxes. It probably would have worried me less if Carter knew where these old papers were and we weren't just knocking around every box trying to find them.

"Do you want me to help?" I kicked one cardboard box and was surprised by how heavy it felt. It didn't budge an inch, not that I was actually trying to move it. It made me wonder what was in all these boxes. What would a frat house store that wasn't beer and red plastic cups?

Carter shook his head. "Nah, I don't think the brothers would like someone going through their stuff. Plus, you might spill all our secrets and I can't have that be on me." He straightened up and moved to open another box. "You still haven't convinced me you're trustworthy, and you *do* look suspicious."

Ha!

"I look suspicious? You brought me down to the basement in an empty house." I folded my arms in front of me.

Carter wasn't even trying to look innocent. He walked over, stopping rather close to me. "Yea... so?"

So? *So?* So... this wasn't what I signed up for. So... this isn't what he should have made me do. So... there was no point in doing this. Were there even any newspapers here?

"Carter, you –" He kissed me quick.

I could feel his hands gently rest on my hips and how Carter kept me close as he took a step closer. I knew that I should push him away and end whatever thing he thought we had going on. It was the only way to protect him, and anyone else in my life. But it felt so nice to be so close to someone else and he was a pretty good kisser. He was making me feel more alive than I had been feeling in the longest time. Maybe I should have been dating this whole time, just to find him.

My arms wrapped around his back to pull us closer until we were flush. I realized I wanted more with him. I wanted to rip that shirt off him and throw away those pants. My body had decided and, even if I regretted this later, I could fix it. I just needed to feel him. My hands snuck under his shirt and drifted up along his back. I could imagine clinging to him, digging my nails into him, while he moved inside me. Him kissing me now just drew up that whole fantasy in brilliant clarity.

His lips moved to my neck and I could do nothing except lean my head back to grant him more access. I wanted to feel those lips on me. I wanted to feel them everywhere. His hand slipped between us and fumbled around with the front of my jeans. Then I heard a loud bang.

I froze. Carter froze. There was another bang and a thud coming from upstairs.

"Hey! Anyone here?"

My mind had gone back to that night. Someone was in this house when no one should have been around. They were going to search the whole house and then find us trapped down here. While there were boxes to write on and dust to write in, I just couldn't get any words out. Carter would see my secret and it would ruin what we could have had. If we were going to die anyways, I didn't want it to be with someone that would hate me. He'd be disgusted by the truth. I'd rather Carter never know and let me spend my last minutes alive in his arms. Short of hiding in the mess, this was it and...

A frustrated laugh from Carter brushed against me throat. It surprised me that he could laugh at a time like this.

"Fucking Carl," he groaned. Carter hadn't made a move to step away I realized, as my thoughts started being sane again. I could definitely feel how much he didn't want to do that. "We gotta go up or he'll hunt the whole house to make sure no one catches him doing weed."

I don't know why Carter told me that. Now I knew that this Carl guy was a pothead. Not that I cared about that. I cared that this pothead had interrupted something

I really wanted – something we both needed – and made me go temporarily crazy.

Carter seemed to sense that and at least had the decency to look sorry. It wasn't like this was his fault though. "We might as well head up. I don't think the pledges left any papers down here after all."

His hand slipped down into mine before he moved away. As Carter lead me back upstairs towards his annoying frat brother, he paused. "Haley, let me take you out this weekend. It'll just be you and me."

I was going to have to wait. Because we couldn't do anything now – not unless we snuck up into his room and I disappeared before anyone could shame me or tease Carter about it later – it seemed there was no choice. I didn't want to just walk away from Carter right now.

I passed him on the stairs, giving him a quick peck on the lips as I moved around him. "Sounds like a date."

Epilogue

"Yesterday, Ayoshi Hora was found by police officers on the Hudson River. Hora was reported missing after being knocked overboard from his upstate yacht earlier this week. Officers located the boat on Oneida Lake, which contained 10,000 kilos of cocaine and over a thousand dollars in counterfeit money.

"Hora is the second person of interest linked to the drug trafficking ring to be identified this month. Last week, Evan "Little Finger" McGarrett was detained at a routine traffic stop and openly admitted all crimes and his connections.

"In a strange series of events, it appears to this reporter, the world is getting a little bit better place to be."

More to Come...

CHAPTER ONE

The bed springs were creaking loudly, probably waking her neighbors at this early hour. But that thought couldn't stop what was going on in the bedroom. Cora knew pain, but she also knew pleasure. And she wasn't one to stop short. Each loud creak cheered her on and only stopped after she gave it one last hurrah. With the last bit of strength, the button on her jeans slid into the hole and it was over. The zipper gave in next. As she sat up, Cora remembered her explicit interactions with a foot long meatball sandwich, a chocolate milkshake and a side order of French fries. Worst of all was her lethargic end to the night passed out on the futon. Now she was forced to deal with the slight digging in of fabric around her midsection for an entire day. But she smiled proudly in the mirror as she tried to tame the wild mess now atop her head. At least she managed to squeeze into the jeans. That was enough of a victory today.

Of course, today was more or less a day to herself, but there were still errands to run. After all the years of watching her mother calmly tend to four children, run a household and keep the finances straight, you'd think that Cora would have this under control. But at twenty-six and single, all that was in her refrigerator was an open jar of pickles and leftover Chinese take-out from at least two weeks ago. The cupboards bore a similar resemblance to a barren food wasteland. But today, that was on the list to remedy. Well, given that there were still funds in her rather depleted bank account to solve that. Nights at the club and moving to an apartment closer to her job in the city didn't provide any buffer. But she was due for a raise... a year ago.

Cora grabbed her clutch purse to deposit the abused checkbook. With a quick stop at the mirror on the wall next to the door to make sure nothing went array in the last five minutes, she was out the door and into the brisk March morning. But brisk almost seemed like an understatement today. She turned down Atlantic Avenue, towards the bank on the corner. It offered a nice reprieve from the chill as she waited in line. For seven in the morning, it just felt like more people should still be sleeping so that the lines would be shorter, and so Cora could get the day's tasks done quickly.

Even though she had worked in this city for a few years now, the people here still didn't seem to align with her personality that much. At first, it had been the slight accent from the southern end of the state but that quickly disappeared to the tiny tang in her dictation. Daily bouts of jesting had been a good motive to adapt.

The line seemed to evaporate in the time Cora was lost in her thoughts. She stepped up to the bank teller and surrendered the checkbook. It was a little trying on the nerves to wait as the woman typed in numbers or codes or chatted on an instant message service. Really, how long could it take to look up one number? Cora just needed to know now if she could get anything other than dime packets of Ramen noodles. The idea of all that sodium seemed to shrink her jeans from the non-existent water retention.

"The balance of your account is three hundred dollars and eighty two cents. Are you planning on making a deposit or withdrawal?" The teller was polite, but that was her job. Most likely she stood there secretly judging Cora. What was it this time? Single Latina mother struggling on Welfare or maybe the nightly street walker? Not that Cora dressed provocative. Her last boyfriend was the bearer of the unfortunate news that she had a look-a-like, whom just happened to be in the porn industry. Not even the fact that Cora wore black horn rimmed spectacles swayed the stereotypes and judgmental comments to her favor. In fact, maybe they worsened the case. *"Long Johnson's Highrise"* was the film that said ex-boyfriend brought over for a 'romantic' evening, hoping to score some roleplay. That hadn't gone well for him.

"Withdrawal." Now the problem was a matter of amount. Rent was just paid and there were only a few bills expected before her next paycheck. "A hundred." It was a nice number. It sounded to anyone bothering to listen like she was taking out something less than a third of her whole bank account. The teller counted it out in twenty dollar bills before slipping it into an envelope and passing it through the slot in the window. Cora stored it for now in the clutch. She took one last warm, deep breath inside the hall of riches before heading out in chilling day.

The supermarket was the last stop on her errands list. Mostly because she didn't want to tote her groceries in the department store while she had tried on shoes, tops, pants in a slightly bigger size. Not that it would have mattered today. There was nothing on the racks or hangers that were worth another glance from Cora.

She grabbed a hand basket at the door and made a left once she made it pass the shopping carts and the registers. There was a short list of basics that were added to the basket – wheat bread, milk, eggs, oatmeal. She laughed to herself when she unconsciously ended up in the isle where the Ramen noodles were stocked. It had to be the frequency that this isle saw of her and not her subconscious body cravings.

Needless to say, she was in a fairly good mood from knowing there'd be more substance in her diet and lack of bloating from copious amounts of sodium. She headed towards the meat counter. Cora thought she deserved to splurge once. There were quite a few choices and she hadn't thought of what she'd make. She knew to only pick up one package because the smell of raw meat was enough of a turn off that she had been flirting with vegetarianism.

Cora picked up a package of Italian sausage, thinking pizza would be a wonderful change to get back into the world of eating. Plus it could last two days if she didn't splurge and inhale the whole meaty pie in one sitting. She reached for a package when a voice spoke out.

"I see you're liking the sausage."

She turned to see an attractive young guy. The dark haired god was probably just under six feet tall and built like a dream. Her best friend, Clarice, would probably wager a bet that he had the sexy vee in his hips and a treasure trail that led down to the biggest dick ever. Clarice would probably go on about the sexcapades and trouble she could get into with this one. Cora just knew that this was probably the corniest pick-up line she ever heard.

"Well, it *is* the best thing to top a pizza."

The guy's lips pulled up into a smirk. "Topping, huh?" Just the way he said it oozed sexual innuendoes. I hadn't caught on sooner, but the truth made me out to be the pizza. The truth sucked. Ah, shit. Now sexy man had my mind in the gutter. "Is that an invitation?"

"Oh, god, no."

His expression just went blank and he stared at her like she had three heads and was covered in neon feathers. Then he busted his gut laughing. "Good one. You had me going there." He reached out his hand. "Dylan Haggerty."

"Uh." This was definitely awkward. Cora wanted to slap away his hand for laughing at her. She had been dead serious. But when was the last time a hot guy took interest in her? Shit, that was it. Cora stuck out her hand and took his. "Cora Valencia."

That sexy smile came back to his face. "Pleasure." Oh, god. Cora was sure it could be. "How about you let me take you out. Dish out some pizza action."

Guess guys nowadays were extra bold and blunt. Too bad she wasn't up and ready for a tumble in bed with all kinds of... toppings. Cora knew she wasn't one that really cared for that kind of thing. Her ex only got as far as one pregnancy scare after "forgetting" to pull out.

"Forget the pizza." And any kind of sex plans he was thinking about. "Ever play mini-golf?"

Again, Dylan laughed. Seriously, was she really that much of a joke? It made her believe that her ex may have been onto something when she stopped fooling around with him. All those things he had said and called her. There was a reason no other man had shown interest, and it wasn't just because she was a fashion whore and half broke. Her curvy size 14 hips and five foot stature had something to do with it.

"You are just a bundle of surprises, huh?" He was shaking his head, but there was a mischievous smile on his face. Before Cora could figure out what he meant, much less get a chance to ask, he said he'd never been. And somehow, it was decided that it would be a date. "Sure. Thursday night. I'll meet you at Cubbie's Putt Putts."

He reached for her hand. It sent a strange tingle along her skin. Why was he affecting her so much? Pulling a pen from his back pocket, he scribbled down seven digits on her palm. "Text me so I can get your digits."

So there was still a way out of this. Dylan had been so sure, so cocky. At the end of it all, it really was Cora's call. She could walk away, finish doing her shopping, and forget his sexy smile and that laugh. Besides, she was pretty sure he was lying right now. If he never played mini-golf, or was too cool for it, then why did he know about the only putt-putt coarse in the city? Maybe she was just assuming he never played, but he definitely wasn't the type that played the sport. Unfortunately, it was one of very few sports that Cora could play without looking like a fool, or a wildebeest shoved into a too-tight sports uniform.

"I'll see ya then, babe." Dylan tossed one more sexy smile her way before grabbing a pack of chicken wings and heading towards the registers.

Who said he could call her babe? That was it. She was blowing off this cocky ass. Cora made sure a package of sausage was in her basket before going to find some cheese to top it all. The day might have started off mediocre and slightly insulting, but it was going to end epically when this pizza got out of the oven. This day was definitely strange and needed to get back on track.

Cora got in line at the registers and waited her turn. She knew these gals had it the roughest. They had to deal with all kinds of bullshit, and probably more guys hitting on them here for discounts on the supersized bag of Doritos and Mountain Dew instead of clipping coupons in their gaming dens. She knew how ridiculous it was to watch unready people fumble with their wallets and then struggle over the concept that of taking their bags of over-priced goodies. Or maybe that was just at her experiences... at her store... at her register.

Her basket was emptied on the conveyor belt. It wasn't a huge haul, but it would get her through another week. Maybe a visit home would be needed so she didn't starve, and that was saying a volumes. Her family was a lot to handle. Starving didn't sound like such a bad way to go after all...

"That'll be ten fifty."

Cora had to shake herself out of her thoughts. She had done one of the things that bothered her the most during her shifts on the register. She apologized as she coughed over the cash. It was hard to hand over that much, especially seeing as her basket was basically a pizza and breakfast for tomorrow morning. Hitting up a Subway for a footlong would have cost her less.

She grabbed her bags and change before making her way back out into the brisk Boston air. It seemed like the city had actually woken up now. Buses and car horns went off every so often. All was in full force. Mobs of suitcase toting beings flooding the crosswalks. And Cora wouldn't want to be anywhere else... at least while as she could make her rent each month.

Kate Sparrows

Kate Sparrows is a Sassy Sue.

She's a cynical hopeless romantic that's in love with her Kindle and book boyfriends. It's really a love that you shouldn't come between. Well, unless you have ice cream, an awesome accent, or an amazing book in your hand. Bonus points having for all three.

Acknowledgements

So this story turned out to be different than my normal romance kind of stuff. Yea, there's a girl in a relationship and out in the world dating, but that's not really the main thing of the story. It's focused on a person with an unusually superpower... because you know, superpowers don't really take work and thought... well, much thought. Okay, so all the other superheroes show up with a plan except Haley. What I'm try to say is, thank you for giving *The Writer* a shot. I am planning to expand it and hopefully you'll enjoy the next chapters in Haley's life.

I want to thank my boyfriend to dragging me along to see *Suicide Squad*. It was the first time I ever heard of The Enchantress... and I knew I wanted to make my own (better) version. The Enchantress seemed almost unstoppable. Haley might truly become unstoppable.

Thank you to each and every one of you that has continued to read my stories. It means a lot to me. You can always reach out and contact me about the books. My contact information has always been at the front of each book, on the copyright page. Feel free to reach out!